Orion William

Kate Walden Directs:
BRIDE OF SLUG MAN

Kate Walden Directs:
BRIDE OF SLUG MAN

Julie Mata

DISNEY • HYPERION
LOS ANGELES • NEW YORK

Printed in the United States of America

First Edition, May 2015
1 3 5 7 9 10 8 6 4 2
G475-5664-5-15074
This book is set in Adobe Caslon.
Designed by Vikki Sheatsley

Library of Congress Cataloging-in-Publication Data
Mata, Julie.
Kate Walden directs : Bride of Slug Man / Julie Mata.—First edition.
pages cm
Sequel to: Kate Walden directs: Night of the zombie chickens.
Summary: A budding middle school movie director juggles her second feature film and her very first crush.
ISBN 978-1-4231-9460-6
[1. Motion pictures—Production and direction—Fiction. 2. Friendship—Fiction. 3. Dating (Social customs)—Fiction. 4. Junior high schools—Fiction. 5. Schools—Fiction.] I. Title. II. Title: Bride of Slug Man.
PZ7.M4239585Kam 2015
[Fic]—dc23 2014028076

Reinforced binding

Visit www.DisneyBooks.com

THIS LABEL APPLIES TO TEXT STOCK

To Daniela and Rebecca,
my wonderful daughters,
who make me laugh

All the cafeteria lunches at Medford Junior High taste like they've been boiled in a rusty cauldron, but the hot dogs are the worst. The cafeteria lady keeps them swimming in a greasy vat of lukewarm water and by the time you bite into one, it's cold and rubbery. Normally, I squirt on globs of mustard and choke it down, but for some reason today I just can't bite into something that looks like a leftover body part. I throw my hot dog down on my tray and it rolls off the stale bun, falls from the table, and bounces on the floor. Alyssa snickers, Lizzy makes a sound like, *yech*, and Margaret grimaces. Doris leans down, picks it up, and puts it back on my bun.

"I am *not* eating that," I inform her. "They're made from cow brains, you know."

Doris blinks at me through her thick lenses. "Actually, hot dogs are a blend of pork, beef, chicken, and turkey. *Not* cow brains." As if to prove her point, she takes a bite of her own and happily munches away. I should know better than to argue with Doris. She's in the gifted program for math and science. Oscar Mayer probably calls her to consult on the chemistry of their wieners.

I steal a potato chip from Alyssa's lunch, glancing around at my friends. They're all busy eating. No one has remembered. And to think I've been nervous all morning, waiting for this moment. Margaret and Doris are talking about their brainiac math teacher's new hairdo. Apparently, it's the square root of ugly. Lizzy and Alyssa are talking about track. Track? Since when are they interested in running around in circles? None of them seems to care that I promised to show them a script from my newest movie project today. I thought for sure someone would have asked about it by now. I guess it's lucky they've forgotten, since I don't have it anyway. I haven't written a single word. Still, the least they could do is seem . . . disappointed.

I chew on a fingernail, since I don't have anything else to eat. Finally, I can't stand it any longer. "So, I guess you guys probably want to know what kind of movie I decided to make."

They all stop talking and gaze at me. Alyssa pops a chip in her mouth. "Oh, yeah, what did you finally decide on?"

I take a deep, dramatic breath. "I'm *completely* stuck. I mean it. I need help."

"Make a zombie sequel," Lizzy says right away.

I finished making my first-ever full-length movie last semester, called *Night of the Zombie Chickens*. I've been telling my friends for weeks that I'm starting a new movie, but the truth is, I'm kind of nervous. I made *Night of the Zombie Chickens* for fun. I figured only my friends and family would see it. Then, my parents rented the old Roxy Theater downtown for a premiere, and the newspaper wrote a story about it. Lots of kids from school and even some teachers came to see it. Now, students come up to me in the hallway and beg to be in my next movie. Everyone wants to know what it's going to be about, which is probably why I have writer's block.

Alyssa makes a face. "No more zombies, please. I'm tired of getting splattered with blood."

"I know!" Margaret says. "Make a musical!"

My eyes bulge at the idea. For *Night of the Zombie Chickens*, I had to work with my mother's evil diva hens, who tried to ruin my life. That was bad enough. But directing a bunch of yowling middle schoolers?

"Sure," I say, always the diplomat. "That could work."

"I thought you were going to make a romance this time," Alyssa says loudly. "Remember?"

I never said the word *romance*. When Alyssa mentioned

it, I didn't say no, either. I guess that sounds like *yes* to a seventh grader who's eager to have a romantic scene with a certain somebody. Alyssa has a secret crush on Jake Knowles, except everyone has pretty much figured it out. Even Jake, probably. Alyssa is the only one who doesn't know that everyone knows. So, like I said, it's a secret.

Doris removes her glasses and polishes them with a greasy napkin. "You should make a movie about dark energy. Did you know that dark energy makes up seventy percent of the universe? You and me and everything on Earth—all the planets and stars everywhere—all the matter, we only make up five percent."

She holds her glasses up to the light. They look even more smeared than before. Margaret snatches them from her and takes a tiny spray bottle from her backpack. She mists the lenses and polishes them with a special cloth, then hands them back. Doris squints through her squeaky-clean glasses and blinks. She's probably never seen the world so clearly before. She peers at us to see if these mind-blowing facts are sinking in. "Isn't that cool?"

"Yeah. Wow." I try my best to look like my mind is blown.

Brave Margaret asks the question the rest of us are avoiding. "So, what *is* dark energy?"

Doris's eyes light up. "It's some kind of mysterious dark force. Einstein predicted that empty space wasn't really empty. That it has its own energy. Scientists think it's pulling the galaxies farther apart. But you can't see it and they can't prove it's really there."

Alyssa leans forward. "Then how would we make a movie about it?" The only dark energy she cares about involves a romantic scene with Jake Knowles.

"You could show a scientist trying to discover this huge mystery of the universe," Margaret offers. "She could sing a song about the stars," she adds dreamily.

Alyssa rolls her eyes. "That sounds thrilling."

"Well, it's more exciting than a romance," Margaret shoots back.

"Well, I vote for werewolves," Lizzy says.

My friends are not much help.

I'm about to jump in before they start arguing, when I see something fly past our heads from the corner of my eye. A moment later, Paul Corbett bellows at the next table. A slimy handful of green beans is sliding down his hair onto his collar.

Our heads snap around to see if Lunch Lady saw what happened. Luckily, she's yelling at some poor sixth grader on the other side of the room. Most of the lunch ladies at our school are moms who volunteer. They have names, like Mrs. Daley or Mrs. O'Neill. Lunch Lady is different. For one thing, no one knows her real name, which is why we have to call her Lunch Lady. There's a rumor she escaped from a loony bin and is hiding out at our school, waiting until the coast is clear. It might be true, because Lunch

Lady is always there and she's always watching us. Her hair is an odd rusty color, permed into little corkscrews, which she keeps flattened to her head with a black net. She has swinging folds of arm flesh and big hammy hands and fingers that remind me of miniature boiled hot dogs. No one misbehaves when Lunch Lady is nearby.

Paul whips his head around and shouts, "Who threw that?" He stares at everyone behind him, searching for a telltale smirk, a guilty face.

Even though we haven't done anything, it's important to *look* like we haven't done anything. Otherwise, Paul might decide to make our lives miserable. Luckily, we're old hands at this. Alyssa is lazily stirring her chocolate milk. Doris is eyeing my hot dog like she might stick it in her backpack for an afternoon snack. Lizzy doodles on a napkin. I'm gazing off into space, nibbling on a potato chip, the kung fu master of humble innocence. Paul's eyes practically scorch us with their glare, but there are a lot of kids sitting behind him and they probably all have their reasons for throwing something at him.

I hate food fights, ever since a chewed-up piece of ketchup-covered hot dog once hit me in the face. Still, if anyone deserves wet, slimy green beans in his hair, it's Paul Corbett. Lizzy has her back to Paul, so she's making funny faces at us, mimicking him. Margaret can't help it; a tiny smile escapes. Big mistake.

Paul's eyes narrow. "What are you laughing at, Margerine? You think it's funny? Did you throw those?"

Paul and Blake Nash pick on a lot of kids, but they keep their worst for Margaret. She's an easy target because she's so nice. Sad to say, but nice can be hazardous to your health in middle school. Plus, she has red hair, freckles, and crooked teeth. She used to be completely ignored until last semester, when she got the lead part in the musical *Annie*. Since then, people have been a little nicer to Margaret, except for Paul. If anything, he's been worse. He points a finger at Margaret. "You're dead, Red." He grabs the beans out of his hair and throws them on the floor.

"Just what do you think you're doing?" a voice bellows. We all freeze. Lunch Lady steams up the aisle, arm flesh flapping, pointing at the beans. "Pick those up right now!" Her mammoth chest heaves with indignation as she glares down at Paul. I'm pretty sure Lunch Lady would protect that lunchroom floor with her last, dying breath.

"Someone threw them at me," Paul whines.

Lunch Lady's face scrunches up even tighter. She's like a teakettle on boil, right before it shoots out steam and starts screaming. Paul jumps up fast and starts picking up beans. Every kid at our table is grinning. It's like the time a guy in a convertible Porsche roared past my dad and me on the highway, probably going a hundred miles an hour. My dad looked mad, but also a little jealous, and grumbled something about rotten drivers. When we saw the Porsche pulled over by a highway patrol car a few miles later, my dad smacked his hands together and waved, grinning, as we drove past. He hummed under his breath for the next fifty miles. It pretty much made his day.

That's how we all feel about Paul getting down on the floor, picking up slimy beans. Finally, justice is served.

The bell rings and we move to dump our garbage. Suddenly, Margaret nudges me. "Look, there's the new boy. His family moved here from New York City."

We all turn and watch as a boy stacks his tray. You can tell right away he's not local. There's something about his clothes and his haircut and his look. I can't figure out exactly what it is. It's just a striped shirt. And it's just some dark blond hair falling into one eye. He's not real tall or big. But somehow, put it all together, and it's one step beyond cool. It's cool without trying to look cool.

I'm so busy staring, I almost miss the garbage can as I toss my spare body part hot dog. "Wow," I murmur.

"Wow," Lizzy agrees.

Doris also gazes at him through her thick glasses. "I just remembered something. I heard he's like you, Kate."

"Wha-at?" I say, stunned. "He likes me?"

I haven't even met the kid! Could he possibly have seen me in the hallway and developed one of those instant crushes? A tiny, secret part of me is thrilled. A cool boy from NYC likes *me*? My mind starts fast-pedaling into the future, imagining our first meeting, shy smiles, my witty remarks, his glowing admiration. In another minute, we'll be married with kids if I don't slow down.

"No, I said he's *like* you," Doris repeats. "I mean, he also likes to make movies, like you."

"Oh. Yeah, I thought that sounded weird." I try to sound nonchalant. Still, it's embarrassing. Lizzy and Alyssa are grinning at each other. My head, which expanded like a hot air balloon, now shrinks smaller than a week-old wiener. Of course he doesn't like me. Why would he? I'm just a boring kid with braces and frizzy brown hair. No boy is ever going to like me, especially with Alyssa standing right next to me. I sigh as I look at her. Tall, perfect teeth, shiny blond hair. She may not understand the scientific theory of dark energy but I'm pretty sure that isn't what seventh-grade boys care about.

I'm just lucky no one heard me except my friends. Someone like Paul Corbett or Tina Turlick might have run over to the new boy and started screaming things like, *Kate Walden thinks you like her! She thinks you have a big crush on her!* Middle school is like that—a series of social land mines just waiting to explode in your face. Even though I know it's unfair, I feel a tiny stab of resentment toward the new boy. What is he, too good for me? I'm not sure which surprises me more, that this kid likes to make movies or that Doris heard and passed along a piece of gossip.

"Really, he makes movies? You actually heard that?"

Doris adjusts her glasses. "Noah Fleming told me in Biology."

Noah Fleming is like Doris reincarnated as a boy. He's a supersmart science geek. He's not bad looking, in a tall, skinny way, but his nerd factor totally outweighs his cute factor. Plus, Paul and Blake stuck him with the unfortunate nickname Nose Phlegmy.

I peer at Doris. "How did Noah hear that?"

"Noah's locker is near Tristan's, so they were talking. I guess Noah mentioned you and your movie. That's his name—Tristan Kingsley."

Tristan. Jeez, even his name is cool. A strange tingling starts in my face. People were talking about me. The new boy from NYC was talking about *me*. He probably did a double take when he heard I've already made a feature-length movie. It *is* just a little impressive. The tingle turns to a warm glow. And then it hits me. Noah's locker is just down from mine. That means Tristan's locker is near mine, too. We can talk movies together. It will be so great to have a filmmaker buddy! A cool NYC filmmaker buddy with blond hair falling in one eye.

I'm still pondering my movie as I head for the bus after school. It's early April and most of the snow has melted into gray slush. I hate my clunky snow boots so I left them at home. Now, the cold slop seeps into my sneakers. By the time I climb on the bus, my feet are soaked. I slide in next to Lizzy and she grins and removes her earbuds.

Lizzy Chang's family moved to Medford when she was in fifth grade. Her parents speak with an accent and Lizzy speaks perfect English and perfect Chinese. Sometimes, just for fun, or when she's mad, she'll talk to herself in Chinese so we don't know what she's saying. We're all good friends but Mimi Reynolds is her BFF. Mimi's family moved to Texas a month ago, so it's been a tough time for Lizzy. She's tiny, even shorter than me. Some people make a mistake and think she's delicate, like a china doll. Really, Lizzy's more like the Great Wall of China. Have a run-in with her and she'll be the last one standing. She's tough and funny and, best of all, she likes making movies.

Olivia Sykes leans forward from the seat behind us. "Anything exciting happen in school today?"

"Why weren't you in gym class?" Lizzy asks.

Olivia pops her gum. "A field trip. We went to the art museum."

"No fair!" Lizzy exclaims. "Why didn't we get to go?"

Olivia shrugs. "It was fun."

Lizzy loves painting and crafty stuff. She can take fabric and whip up a cute toy or purse while the rest of us are still staring at our material, trying to figure out what to do.

Olivia lowers her voice. "Jack Timner got in trouble at the museum today."

Lizzy grins. "What'd he do?"

We both glance toward the back of the bus where Jack sits. He isn't a bad kid, but he can't settle down. He's always trying to be the center of attention. He'll do any stupid thing if he thinks someone will laugh, which lands him in trouble a lot. Jack isn't laughing now, though. His face is sullen, legs splayed out in the aisle. He's probably hoping someone will trip over them.

Jack suddenly looks up and catches my eye, like he knows we're talking about him. He glares and I look away. Both his parents are ex-military. I heard they crack down hard on Jack and have threatened to send him to military school. No wonder he looks glum.

"He pretended like he was going to draw on a painting," Olivia whispers.

I give a delighted gasp of horror. Even I know that is serious. That's like joking on an airplane that you hope the bomb in your suitcase doesn't go off. "Are you kidding? What happened?"

"He was holding up a marker near a painting, trying to be funny for his buddies, and two guards ran over shouting at him. They grabbed him and took him away, and Mr. Graves had to go talk to the museum director. Now Jack can't go on any more field trips and he's got about a month of detentions. They called his parents." Olivia makes a face. "You know what that means."

I risk another glance at Jack. That's when I notice Tristan Kingsley sitting in the seat behind Jack. I quickly turn around. I can hardly believe my luck. The cute moviemaking boy from New York City rides my bus.

Olivia taps me on the shoulder. "So when do you start your next movie? I really want to be a zombie."

"Haven't you heard?" Lizzy says importantly. "No zombies this time. Kate's going to do something completely different. She's just not sure what."

"Oh, I know!" Olivia squeals. "You *HAVE* to do a vampire movie! Vampires would be SO cool. And we could make it really scary. Everyone would want to be in it!"

I try not to roll my eyes. Vampires are so overdone.

"I keep telling her it should have werewolves," Lizzy says. "Werewolves are cool."

"They are," Olivia admits, "but they're too furry. Who wants to look like a rabid dog? Vampires are hot."

The bus chugs up to Lizzy and Olivia's stop. They're still debating werewolves versus vampires as they get off. It's Jack Timner's stop, too. His backpack hits me in the back of the head as he goes by. Probably payback for staring at him. "Sorry," he calls over his shoulder, smirking.

Hot vampires, hairy werewolves—I sigh and lean back. I'm pretty sure Alyssa doesn't want to wear fangs or fur. It's great that so many kids want to be in my movie, but I'm going to need someone to help me control the chaos. I need an assistant. Who would be right for the job? I stare out the window at the bare trees flying past. Gray slush splatters the dirty snow mounded on the curbs as we pass by. Winter always drags on too long, like one of those boring black-and-white foreign films that never ends. I slip off my shoes. My socks are wet and my toes feel like tiny blocks of ice.

The bus slows down as we enter a development on the edge of town. It's called Deer Hollow even though the deer are long gone. This area used to be full of trees but now it's lined with big, fancy houses. We stop at a new home and Tristan swings past and hurries down the bus steps. I watch him walk up the long driveway. What kind of movies has he made? Most likely short ones with his friends. He would probably love to help make a longer movie. That's when it hits me. Tristan would be the perfect assistant director! I may not be a big-time Hollywood player yet, but I can teach him what I've learned so far.

We stop at a few more houses in Deer Hollow until I'm the last person on the bus. Sal, the bus driver, has to drive another ten minutes on country roads to reach my home. I sigh and wish for the millionth time that my family had moved to Deer Hollow instead of a run-down farmhouse in the middle of nowhere. The funny thing is, we have tons of deer. All the ones that got chased off by the mega-house invasion must have headed over to our place.

Sal glances at me through the big mirror over his head. I always feel bad for him because he has a girl's name. He's Italian and I guess it's short for Salvatore. The boys on the bus all call him Sally but he doesn't seem to mind.

"You decided what your next movie's about, Kate?" he calls out. Sal's a big film buff. He even came to my premiere

"I'm not sure. Maybe a romance."

Sal twists his lower lip, like he sucked on a lemon. "Romance? Hmmm. Could be tricky."

"Yeah, I know."

The bus finally wheezes to a stop outside our house and I hurry up the aisle. "Crime drama," Sal says out of the corner of his mouth, like he's offering me a shady tip on a horse race. "Italian mafia. Hasn't been done well since *The Godfather*." He taps his head. "I got all kinds of stories.

From my grandfather, about the old days. Somebody needs to make it into a movie."

This stops me in my tracks. "Your grandfather was in the mafia?"

Sal laughs like this is a funny joke. "No, no, no. Maybe." He shrugs. "He knew people who knew people."

I'm dying to ask Sal if he's in the mafia too, but if he admitted it, then he might have to kill me so I couldn't tell anyone.

"I'll think about it," I promise.

What I'm really thinking about as I swing off the bus is how great it would be to have a cute A.D. from NYC helping me on my next project. The thought warms my insides, all the way down to my frozen feet.

The first thing I see when I get off the bus is a bunch of fat hens waddling through the slush. "You've got to be kidding," I mutter under my breath. My day just took a sharp turn for the worse.

Usually, my mother keeps her chickens inside their coop during cold weather. With some of the snow melting, she probably figured they could spend some time outside. My mother used to have a great job as a business manager. Then she decided to start her own company called Heavenly Hens. She raises organic chickens and sells the meat and eggs to restaurants and health-food stores. They say chickens are harmless, but there's a reason why they're called fowl. As in foul, pesky, and possibly evil. They've had it in for me ever since I made them zombies in my first movie. It was their fault I landed on the loser list for a while last semester. Even now, the hens are cackling and staring at me with their beady eyes, like they're all in on some joke I don't get. And then I see the punch line. Piles of steaming poop dot the yard like mini land mines.

As I walk up the driveway, I practically trip and fall trying to avoid a fresh mound. My mother says the hens poop everywhere because they don't know any better, but they know plenty. They know exactly how much it bugs me. There's nothing worse than chicken poop stuck on the bottom of your shoe. Trust me, I know all about it. I run the rest of the way to the house, avoiding messes and splashing through puddles, until I've escaped safely inside.

"Mom," I yell, "the hens are out in the yard!"

No answer.

The house feels strangely quiet until our terrier, Wilma, explodes into the room. She's so happy, she streaks around the kitchen like a barking, furry missile. At least *someone* is glad to see me. I kick off my wet shoes, peel off my sweatshirt, dump my backpack on the floor, and dive into the fridge. As I emerge with a big, green pickle, I notice a suitcase near the stove. My mother hurries in, dressed up more than usual.

"Hi, Kate, I'm glad you're home. I need to go over a few things with you."

I eye the suitcase. "Are you going somewhere?"

She starts checking things off a to-do list on the counter. "I've got that poultry conference, remember? I told you all about it."

Hazily, I recall her mentioning something about a meeting in Omaha. It didn't occur to me she was actually planning on going. "You mean, you're leaving right now?" I feel a twinge of anxiety. Will our home even function without her? I envision the lights stuttering and shutting off, the hens wasting away, the refrigerator bare except for containers of moldy sour cream.

"The conference doesn't start for a few days, but I got a call today from your grandmother. She's not feeling well so I'm going to stay a couple days with her, then go on to Omaha. I already told your dad."

My mother hands me a brochure. "Here's where I'll be." The brochure reads: *Sixth Annual Organic Poultry Farmers Conference.* Inside, there's a long list of workshops. "'Shell Egg Sanitation,'" I read off, making a face. "'Evaluation of Ingredients in Organic Poultry Nutrition.'" I glance at my mother. She's smiling like I just named off a hit Broadway musical she gets to see. I move on to the next. "'Microbiology and Pathology of Avian Diseases.'"

Wow, just saying it out loud puts my brain in a coma. Four days of talking and hearing about nothing but chickens. Their nasty food, their gloppy eggs, their disgusting diseases. It sounds like a fate worse than death by zombie bite.

"Mom, are you serious?" I blurt. "Is someone making you go to this?"

"Of course not, silly. I want to go." She takes back the printout. "This is a great chance to connect with other organic poultry producers and hear about the latest developments."

Is this what happens when you become an adult? You suddenly become fascinated by the most incredibly boring stuff in the universe? I sigh, feeling sorry for her. Still, maybe it won't be so bad. The last time she visited our grandmother, we had a week of Chinese takeout, late bedtimes, and lots of junk food. "You're right, you should go," I encourage her. "You don't want to miss any exciting developments."

I hear Derek's bus wheeze to a groaning stop outside on the road. A minute later, he bursts in the door.

"I need to make slime!" he announces. "Kate, you want to help me?"

"Slime?" my mother echoes uneasily.

Derek likes to pretend the kitchen is a science laboratory. He has a bad habit of mixing weird things together and then overcooking them in the microwave until they erupt.

"It's an extra-credit assignment for science." Derek shows her a recipe. "My teacher gave it to me."

My mother bites her lip. Still, she can't argue with a homework assignment. "Looks like we have everything you need," she says, glancing over the ingredients. "It should all be in the pantry. Kate, can you supervise, please?"

Derek scowls. "I don't need her to supervise. I know how to cook. I'm a better cook than Kate!"

"Yeah, if you like exploded food," I point out. "Don't worry, I'll make sure he doesn't burn down the house."

My mother glances at her watch. "I really need to go."

Derek's mouth drops open. "Where are you going?"

My mother shakes her head at us. "Don't you two listen to anything I tell you?"

"It's that chicken thing," I tell him. "And she's going to visit Grandma, too."

"Now, I've left a schedule on the refrigerator door for your father. You're both responsible for helping your dad look after the hens. I'll be back Saturday afternoon. And Kate, I'd like you to make dinner tonight. Just spaghetti and salad. I left everything out on the counter."

I nod. How hard can spaghetti and a salad be?

"All right, then." She smiles brightly at us.

Derek's face has been growing longer and longer. When she darts upstairs for some forgotten item, he trails after her like he's suddenly forgotten how to function on his own. "Why do you have to be gone so long?" he whines. "Why can't I go with you? Are you going to bring us something?"

"Have fun," I tell her, even though that doesn't seem likely. She looks excited, though, like she's going on vacation. In a way, I guess she is. No cooking or cleaning for five days. She hugs us and we stand at the door and wave as she pulls out.

Derek sighs, looks dejected for a second, then turns and grins at me. "Let's make slime!"

"Sure." I grab the recipe from him, and that's when I notice he's wearing his Spytech Super Sleuth Wristwatch. For the last few months, Derek has been obsessed with spying. He's always been a bit of a sneak, but now he's decided to make a career out of it. He got the watch and some other spy gear for Christmas. His top priority lately is to catch me doing something embarrassing.

"If I'm going to help you, then take that thing off." I point to the watch. It shoots video with sound, so I'm not taking any chances. "No spying allowed."

"Fine." Derek makes a big show of pulling off the watch and sticking it in a drawer. "Happy now?"

"Yes." I glance at his recipe. "Condensed milk and cornstarch? That's it? This should be easy."

Derek grabs the ingredients from the pantry and dumps the canned milk into a saucepan. I measure out the cornstarch and let him stir it in. Slowly, the milk starts to thicken. After a while, Derek lifts the spoon and a stream of gooey liquid slides off it.

"It worked!" he says. "We made slime! This is so cool!" He suddenly pulls a pair of sunglasses out of his pocket, puts them on, and gazes at the concoction. "Hmm," he says. "Interesting."

The sunglasses have clunky, black frames. They look like

something our grandmother might wear. "Uh, what are you doing?" I ask.

"I'm just seeing if this stuff looks any better if it's darker." He takes the pot off the heat. "I think what it needs is food coloring. Quick, grab the green before it cools off!"

With a few drops of green coloring, the whitish goo suddenly looks a lot more like slime. After it's cooled, Derek grabs a handful and squeezes until it oozes between his fingers. "It looks like the slime from those gross slugs in Mom's garden." He grins at me and intones, "Slug Man is on the loose, spewing slime across Megatropolis."

Yeah, it's kind of silly, but the slime is too tempting. I grab some. It feels wonderfully gloppy and gooey. I affect an old-time radio voice: "Slug Man, spawned in the murky mire of planet Mars, turns his victims into mollusks with venomous goo!" Just for fun, I throw a blob against the wall. It leaves a green trail as it slides down, just like a slug. Derek chortles. "Try it!" I tell him.

He hesitates. "What about Dad?"

"He won't know. Come on, it's fun!"

Derek shakes his head. "I don't think you should do that. It might stain."

"Stain? Are you kidding?" I pick up another handful of ooze and throw it against the wall, where it lands with a pleasing splat. Just then, a brilliant thought bursts across my brain like a flaming Roman candle on the Fourth of

July. SLUG MAN! It would make the perfect sci-fi flick! A mutant slug from Mars spews slime, transforming victims into fellow slug creatures. "Wow," I murmur. And then I shout, "WOW!"

Derek thinks I'm excited about the slime balls, but I'm thinking about my next movie. I've always wanted to try a special effects scene with a flying saucer. Plus, I'll get to make gallons of gooey, green slime. I might even need to whip up some blood if Slug Man turns out to be a carnivore.

Normally I don't tell Derek my movie ideas, but I'm so excited I can't help myself. "Hey, Derek, how does this sound? I'm thinking about having a slug man character in my next movie."

Derek's face lights up. "Hey, that's my idea! I thought up the name!"

"I know. Good job."

"Can I be Slug Man?!"

"No, you're too short. But maybe you can be a victim."

"So, what is a slug man?" he asks doubtfully. "I mean, what would he do?"

"I don't know yet. But he'll definitely spew slime. Maybe he'll want to take over the world."

Derek puts the rest of his slime in a plastic container to take to school as I wipe the mess off the floor. I'm in such a good mood, I almost reach out and tousle his hair like I used to do when we were little. He was such a cute kid, back when he adored me and followed me everywhere. When he was a toddler, he called me Kee-Kee because he couldn't say my name. Now, he calls me Warthog, and if I tousled his hair he would probably yell at me. As I give the floor a last wipe, a terrible thought hits me. There's nothing romantic about an extraterrestrial trying to rule the world. What will Alyssa think?

Derek notices my frown. "What's the matter?"

"Alyssa wants me to make . . . something different." I catch myself just in time. Alyssa would kill me if I divulged too much to Derek.

"I bet she wants to be all romantic kissy-face with somebody, right?" Derek makes smacking noises with his lips. Sometimes he isn't as dumb as I like to think he is. He shrugs. "Just do like Frankenstein."

"Frankenstein? What are you talking about?"

Derek takes the bowl of slop that we've mopped off the floor and dumps it in the sink. "The monster in Frankenstein got a bride in the sequel, remember? He loved her, she hated him. Instant romance. Barf."

I stare at him. Not only is Derek not dumb; sometimes, he's scarily close to brilliant.

It turns out I was right. Spaghetti is easy to make. I add the pasta to the pot of water and put it on the stove to boil. While it's cooking, I throw some lettuce in a bowl, add a few cherry tomatoes, and pour dressing on top. Once the pasta is done, I turn off the heat and leave it on the stove. Finally, I dump the spaghetti sauce into a pan to heat.

I run upstairs, turn on my computer, and sit down. I need to write a script while the idea is still fresh in my head. Alyssa can play the girl who Slug Man falls in love with. Still, I don't think she'll want to get romantic with a slime-spewing extraterrestrial. She's pretty picky about her hair. Anyway, why would a beautiful girl fall in love with a gruesome gastropod guy? I rub my temples, thinking hard.

Maybe she's blind. Or she's got a thing for aliens? Then it hits me. It's so simple! I know just how to write it to keep Alyssa happy. There's even a singing part for Margaret. I furiously type:

EXT: ADRIENNE'S YARD—DAY

WILMA the TERRIER trots across a wide, grassy farmyard out in the country. A few CHICKENS cluck nearby. Suddenly, Wilma's head snaps up. She sniffs the breeze, then races across the yard, BARKING like crazy. The chickens scatter.

CUT TO:

A silver FLYING SAUCER shoots across the sky, alien lights blinking. It stops and hovers over the yard. Wilma backs away, GROWLING, as the flying saucer slowly touches down.

CUT TO:

CLOSE-UP of a strange creature stepping out of the saucer's door. It looks part SLUG, part MAN. The SLUG MAN approaches the farmhouse. He hides behind a bush as the front door opens and out steps . . . ADRIENNE, in a white wedding dress. It's her wedding day!

Slug Man does a double take when he beholds the beautiful Adrienne. He draws dangerously closer. If she looked up, she might see him. From his pocket, he pulls out a photo of a SLUG CREATURE that looks just like him, except it has more hair and wears a pink bow. He crumples the photo in his hand and throws it on the ground, then stares at Adrienne, making a lonely, CROAKING sound. Suddenly, he HISSES and backs off, as Adrienne's bridesmaid, SHANNON, joins her.

SHANNON

Christopher's a lucky man! But we need to go or you're going to be late for your own wedding!

Adrienne and Shannon get into a car and drive off. Slug Man turns and hurries back toward his ship.

CUT TO:

The silver flying saucer takes off, lights flashing, and whirls away.

I push back from my computer. It's a good start. The next scene will be the wedding. Margaret can sing a song and the bride and groom will share a kiss, right before Slug Man breaks in and turns Christopher into a slug creature. I'll make sure Alyssa and Jake rehearse a couple times. I'll let Margaret pick the song she's going to perform and Doris can be in charge of outfitting the scientists who track down Slug Man. That should keep all my friends happy except Lizzy, because, as hard as I try, I can't figure out how to work a werewolf into the script.

"Something's burning!" Derek calls.

I rush downstairs. The spaghetti sauce is boiling like crazy and half of it has splattered all over the stove.

My dad walks in as I'm cleaning it up. His thinning hair looks rumpled and his tie hangs crooked. Must have been a rough day.

"Hi, Dad, dinner's ready. I made it all by myself."

He pecks me on the head. "Smells great. Let me change and then we can eat."

I set the table and call Derek, who's outside spying on the chickens. As we sit down, my dad rubs his hands together. "Looks wonderful, Kate."

Actually, the dinner isn't even close to wonderful. It turns out that cooking is a little harder than I thought. The sauce is burned and the noodles are fat as worms from sitting in the water too long. Even the salad wilted. I guess you're not supposed to put the dressing on two hours ahead of time.

"It's delicious," my dad says in his fake hearty voice. He plows through the watery pasta and burned sauce, but I can only stand a few mouthfuls. I'm a failure as a chef.

"I wish Mom were here," Derek mutters. He pushes the spaghetti around on his plate.

"What do you mean?" Dad leans back in his chair and gazes at us. "We're going to have lots of fun this week, right?"

"Kate shouldn't be cooking," Derek insists. "This is terrible." He shoots a crafty look at me. "And she makes big messes."

I hoot. "Me? Look who's talking!"

Derek raises his eyebrows. "Maybe we should review the evidence."

Suddenly, he whips out his mini-tablet. It must have been

hidden in his lap. He hooks a cable up to it and then plugs the other end of the cable into his sunglasses.

Wha-at? Since when do sunglasses have plug-ins? I lean forward for a closer look, just as a grainy video appears on the screen. It's me, standing in the kitchen, throwing a slime ball. We watch as it hits the wall with a wet splatter. Uh-oh. Somehow, seeing it makes it more official. More punishable. I need to launch a quick counterassault.

"Dad! He's videotaping me behind my back! That is so illegal!"

"It's not behind your back," Derek protests. "See? You're looking right at me." He fast-forwards to the part where I throw the second slime ball. I hear Derek's voice: "What about Dad?"

And then my own: "He won't know. Come on, it's fun!"

If Derek's grin were any wider, it would split his face in two. My dad turns and looks at me. Big uh-oh. "Kate, why are you throwing that wet . . ." He flaps his hand, trying to describe it.

"It's a slime ball, Dad," Derek pipes up.

"Yes, why are you throwing those slime balls at the wall?"

"Uh, I was helping with Derek's science experiment. Mom asked me to help him."

"I was just supposed to make slime. I never said anything about throwing it," Derek says in his fake concerned voice.

He's good. It's time to call in the heavy artillery. I reach deep down and pull out my biggest gun—the Puppy Face. It's a risky strategy. Overuse of the Puppy Face has been known to backfire. Still, my back's against the wall. Big eyes. Tremulous voice. "Is he allowed to spy on me now, just to try and get me in trouble?" I open my hands, palms up, appealing to a Higher Authority. "I was just having a little fun, that's all. And I cleaned it up afterward."

Derek is still grinning impishly at me. He's probably been dreaming of this moment for days. His main joy in life is seeing me embarrassed or in trouble. My dad rubs his eyes. He's probably wishing my mother were here, too. He points at the tablet.

"Derek, turn that thing off. Number one—" He holds up a finger. "If you are going to use those toys to spy on your sister, then those toys are going to be taken away. Understood?"

The smile slides off Derek's face. My dad turns to me. "Kate, you're the oldest. I expect more mature behavior than what I just saw. You should be providing your brother with an example, not egging him on."

I gaze down at my plate and nod. A good point, duly noted. What I really want to know is, where did those sunglasses come from? I know Derek didn't get them for Christmas or his birthday. I sneak a quick peek at them. They look kind of dorky, but I'm impressed because they look pretty normal, too. I wouldn't have guessed they were hiding a camera with a mike. Finally, I can't stand it any longer. "Derek, where did you get those?"

He grins slyly at me. "I bought them with birthday money. Fooled you, didn't I?"

Derek has won this skirmish, hands down. I grin back at him. "Pretty slick."

Still, I'm not thrilled that he has yet another spy toy. It's bad enough I have a nosy brother. Now, I have a nosy brother with hidden recording devices. Derek is acting like he would never think of spying on me again, but I know better. It's like asking a slug not to ooze slime. From now on, I need to be on my guard.

It's time to change the conversation, before my dad decides to tack on an extra lesson-learner, like no TV for a while. I quickly tell him my movie idea. He nods as I explain what I've written so far.

"Sounds like fun, Kate. And I love the title." He bravely takes another bite of spaghetti. "What is your slug man going to look like?"

Hmmm. I hadn't even thought about that. A good costume will be critical. I don't want him looking like a Muppet from Mars. It looks like I need to do some research.

After dinner, we all troop into my dad's office. I sit down at his computer and type in *mollusk costume*. I'm surprised by how many hits come back. Apparently, lots of people want to dress up like slugs. The first couple are homemade outfits that look more silly than scary.

"Look!" Derek points to a headline that reads: *Slug Horror Costume.*

I click on it and up pops the perfect getup. The body is long and brown, made of a shiny fabric so it appears wet. The mask looks devilish, with tiny eyeholes and fangs. Two horns stick out from the head. It has long sleeves and two evil-looking claws, which are actually gloves.

"Whoa," Derek says. "That is a cool Halloween costume."

My heart lifts. "That," I say, "is Slug Man."

I glance at the price—fifty dollars. Ouch. Still, I have the cash I collected at my premiere. If I'm going to be a Hollywood director, I have to get used to spending lots of money.

I get my hoard of cash and carefully count out fifty dollars. Then I pull out another twenty for the special two-day delivery. I still have plenty left in my budget and right now even two days seems like a long time to wait. I hand the money to my dad so he can order with his credit card.

"It's pretty pricey." He looks at me. "Are you sure it's worth it?"

I gaze at the slick brown costume. It's perfect. Anyway, a big-budget film deserves a big-budget wardrobe item. "Oh, yeah," I say. "It's worth it."

Romance is about to meet sci-fi, with a slimy twist.

The next day at school I can hardly wait to tell Alyssa my movie idea. I'm hurrying toward my locker before first period when she catches up with me.

"Hey, did you finish the Language Arts assignment?"

I groan. I spent the entire night before jotting down ideas for my movie. I forgot all about homework. "Was that due today?"

"You're in trouble," Alyssa says cheerfully.

"I'm starting to get a stomachache," I joke. "I might have to spend Language Arts class in the nurse's office."

Margaret joins us just as we spot the group of kids hanging out near my locker. As usual, Lydia Merritt is in the center of them all. Lydia has a big mouth but it looks good on her. It gives her a megawatt smile. She has matching big lungs, which give her a megawatt voice. Her most loyal hangers-on, Tina Turlick, Sara Gonzalez, and Emily Foster, are laughing at every word that falls from her mouth.

Some of the guys are there, too—Jack Timner, Jake Knowles, and Paul and Blake. Then, I notice Tristan Kingsley. He's right in the middle of things, talking to Lydia. How did he manage that? Breaking into middle-school cliques is like trying to crack open a big safe. Even dynamite won't get you in. You've got to be skillful enough to pick the lock. This Tristan kid is good, I'll give him that.

Alyssa spots Jake and quickly fluffs her hair. She laughs loudly, even though I haven't said anything. "Look who's talking to Lydia," she says under her breath.

I nod to show I've seen Tristan. Or maybe she meant Jake. My pulse rate quickens. To an adult, it might look like we're just walking up to a group of kids. Actually, we're multitasking. We're scanning faces for friendly looks, assessing risk, listening to hear the conversation thread, all while pretending not to notice them, in case they ignore us. It's hard work first thing in the morning. Suddenly, Lydia wheels around and bawls, "There she is!" and points my way. I'm so surprised, I almost look behind me to see who she's pointing at. "This is our very own Hollywood director," Lydia announces. "Hollywood, have you met New York?" She points at Tristan.

I stick my hands in my pockets and strike a nonchalant pose. "Hey."

"Hey," he counters.

"This is *the* Kate Walden," Lydia informs him. She waves a hand in his direction. "This is Tristan. Kate made the zombie movie we were telling you about."

Everyone is nodding and looking at me. Suddenly, I get what's going on. They want to show this hip New York kid that Medford Junior High is cool, too. The very thought makes me laugh. Still, I'm flattered. It's nice they're treating me like I'm somebody important. I guess I *am* the only kid in school who's made an entire movie.

"She had a premiere at the theater downtown," Sara chimes in. "They even wrote it up in the newspaper."

Wow. Who knew I would stroll into school this morning and suddenly be famous? I shrug humbly like, no big deal.

"Alyssa was the star," Lydia exclaims. "Let me tell you, this girl can scream!"

Now it's Alyssa's turn to smile modestly.

"Yeah, show us how you scream, Alyssa," Paul says. "Do it right now!"

Alyssa gives him a withering look. "Yeah, right. Like I want to spend the afternoon in detention."

"I'll be there," Paul jokes. He turns to Tristan. "I paper-bombed one of the toilets."

This is when I'm pretty sure I like Tristan. He doesn't laugh or say *cool.* He just gives Paul a pained smile, like he wants to ask, *And you thought that was a good idea?* And what is it about that thatch of hair falling into one eye?

Margaret ducks her head next to me and inspects the notebooks she's carrying. I realize nobody introduced her to Tristan or said a word to her. They all still ignore her like she doesn't even exist. Not too long ago, I wouldn't have given it a second thought. I've been ignored plenty myself lately, though. I know how it feels. The thing is, if I introduce Margaret, will Paul embarrass her by calling out one of his stupid nicknames? Wouldn't that be worse than being ignored? I'm still trying to decide when Tristan turns to me and says, "I'd love to see your movie some time."

"Sure," I say lightly. Inside, I'm doing a fist pump. Last semester, all these kids were either ignoring me or making fun of me. Now, it's like I'm one of them. Not that I care. But it's nice to be appreciated. "So you're interested in making movies?"

Tristan looks up and I notice his eyes are blue. Bright, swimming pool blue. "Yeah, what directors do you like?"

"Uh . . ." Everybody's looking at me. Even Lydia is waiting to hear. Think fast. "Hitchcock, of course. . . ."

Tristan nods. "Totally. Love *Psycho*."

"Tim Burton, George Lucas." It feels great to talk like a film expert and have everybody hang on my words.

He grins. "Yeah, you gotta love *Star Wars*."

"There are lots of great directors." Actually, I'm blanking out right about now. I'm not used to so many pairs of eyes staring at me. "How about you?"

"Well, I like those guys. I also kind of go for the European art cinema directors. And French New Wave."

He throws this out with complete casual. Seriously, European art cinema? French New Wave? Who is this kid? Everyone is staring at him, eyes glazed. Whatever he said, it sounds cool. I wish I knew what he was talking about.

"Oh, yeah," I answer. "French New Wave is awesome."

Time to change the subject, before he asks me to name my favorite French New Wave movie.

"So I'm going to be working on another movie soon. You could help if you want." I glance around the circle. Everyone looks interested. Maybe I'll have two assistants for this movie. I can get a megaphone and sit on my director's chair and shout orders at everyone. That would be fun. "Making a feature-length is a lot different than working on little five-minute movies," I explain. "There's a lot of planning. Preproduction meetings, storyboards, continuity, that kind of thing."

Okay, I'm showing off a little, throwing out every movie term I can think of. A storyboard is a series of drawings for each scene. I only did one for *Night of the Zombie Chickens*. I ended up pitching it after Derek said it looked like a six-year-old drew it. Preproduction meetings consisted of Alyssa and me lounging in my bedroom arguing over who should play the next zombie and how they should die. Still, it sounds impressive. I'm going to have kids fighting each other over parts.

"You can be my assistant director if you want," I tell Tristan. "I can show you some of the stuff I've learned." That should thrill him. I had to learn everything the hard way and here I am offering to take him under my wing.

He's nodding as if he's interested. "What's your next film about?"

I wasn't expecting that question. My heart starts to hammer. The last thing I want to do is explain the idea in front of everybody. The whole group is waiting to hear. I can't say I don't know; that would sound stupid. I clear my throat. "My first movie was horror. So I decided to go sci-fi this time."

From the corner of my eye, I see Alyssa's eyebrows shoot up. I can almost hear her thinking, *Sci-fi? What happened to romance?* Margaret looks puzzled, too. She's probably wondering if there's such a thing as a sci-fi musical.

"But with a twist," I hurry on. "A love story. So a sci-fi romance."

Tristan nods. Everyone else nods. "So what's the title?"

Now that it comes to it, I feel a little funny saying *Bride of Slug Man*. It doesn't sound very European artsy. Maybe I got a little too carried away with Derek last night, throwing slime at the wall. It all sounded so fun. Now, in front of my classmates, I'm not so sure. Still, a director has to believe in her own project. She has to have a vision, even if no one else gets it.

I clear my throat again. "I decided to call it . . . *Bride of Slug Man.*"

I scan the crowd. Confused faces. "It's about this slug creature that lands on Earth from Mars," I go on hurriedly. "He falls in love with this woman, so he tries to kidnap her and he ends up changing her husband into a slug creature, too. And he shoots toxic slime at people. . . ." My voice falters. It sounded so different when I thought it up last night. Now, it sounds silly. "That's all I have so far," I mutter. I can feel the blood rushing to my face.

Tristan is giving me that same pained smile he gave Paul . . . *And you thought that was a good idea?* He flips the hair out of his eyes. "Sounds like a cross between *Mars Needs Moms* and *King Kong.*"

Mars Needs Moms? That movie just happens to be one of the biggest box-office flops in history. That's what he's comparing my movie to? He makes it sound like I'm ripping off other people's ideas. I should have known. This kid is just another East Coast snob. Hasn't he heard? There are no new ideas. The same old ones just get recycled over and over. I'm pretty sure someone famous said that once.

"*Slug* Man?" Blake repeats. He snickers. "Your movie's about a *slug*?"

"An alien," I retort. "Like in the movie *Super 8*, or *Cowboys and Aliens.*"

"You know, that sounds like fun," Tristan says. "I'd like to help out, but I'm going to be working on my own movie. A crime drama. Kind of film noir-ish."

Film noir. Dang. That's one of my favorite movie genres. It's a style from the 1940s and '50s in black-and-white, full of criminals, con men, and dangerous dames.

"It's called *Belly of the Naked Beast*," he adds.

Jack Timner leans forward. "*That* sounds cool." It's amazing how someone can insult you without even looking your way. I feel like my feet weigh fifty pounds each and they're stuck to the floor.

"Does it have a naked lady?" Paul asks.

Tristan ignores him. "It's about a detective and a mysterious high-society girl. And there's going to be some epic gun battles."

My movie already sounds lame and his sounds awesome. How did he turn the tables on me so quickly? This kid is good. Good and annoying.

"Cool!" Lydia practically shouts. "I want the part of the mysterious high-society girl!"

"I'm holding auditions this Saturday," Tristan says. "We'll start shooting the following weekend."

Auditions? That sounds so . . . professional.

"I'm going to need a lot of gangsters for the gunfights," he adds.

All the guys perk up. It's amazing how the word *gunfight* gets their blood pounding.

I need to do something quick or there won't be anyone left to be in my movie. "Well, that's funny because, uh, it just so happens that my first day of shooting is this Saturday. And you don't have to audition to be in my movie. Anyone who wants to be in it should text me and I'll give you directions to my house."

Nobody looks excited.

"Oh, good," Paul says. "I always wanted to be a slug!"

A few titters swirl around me but I can't tell who's laughing. My face is heating up like a stove burner.

"So, where are you submitting your film?" Tristan asks me.

It must be a trick question. I have no idea what he's talking about, so I shrug. He's definitely trying to make me look stupid in front of everybody.

"I found one festival that's in June." Tristan flips the hair out of his eyes again. That gesture is starting to bug me. "The Big Picture Film Festival. It's only an hour from here, in the city. They have a Young Filmmaker category. Last year, my movie won the second-place student award at a festival in New York."

Film festivals. Of course. I should have thought of that. So he already made a film? And it won a prize? My head is reeling. I can feel some of the kids glance my way and I know what they're thinking. *My* movie hasn't won any awards.

"Wow, that is so awesome," Lydia says. "You should

have a party and do like a marathon screening and show us your movies."

Tristan grins. "Sure, why not?"

"Sounds like he doesn't need to work on your slug movie, Crapkate," Paul sneers.

I freeze at the mention of my dreaded nickname. The sudden burning in my chest feels all too familiar. It was only a few months ago that Paul cursed me with that nickname, all because some dried chicken poop fell off my shoe at school. For a while, everyone was calling me that. What if I become the butt of a fresh round of jokes? Just like that, I've gone from Medford Junior High's star student to a dud. The stunning speed of my rise and even faster fall has my head spinning. Who does this Tristan guy think he is, coming in and making me look bad? Here I wanted to help him, show him the ropes, and he's . . . I can't exactly explain what he's doing, but it's irritating.

"That's funny," I say loudly. "I was planning on entering the Big Picture Film Festival, too. What a coincidence."

"Hey, it'll be like a contest," Tina Turlick says. "Who's gonna win the top prize?"

Tristan smiles like he's already got it wrapped up. "You have to register online," he tells me, as if I'm a newbie who doesn't know anything. "If you need help with it, let me know."

Like I'm some kind of dummy who can't figure out an online registration form! I'm about to say something incredibly scathing yet witty when the bell rings. I notice a couple of guys jostle each other to walk next to Tristan. Margaret waves and heads off to class. I never even had a chance to introduce her. Things went downhill so quickly. Lockers slam and everyone else hurries away, too. Except for Alyssa. She's staring at me like I'm a big slug she'd like to squish.

Alyssa folds her arms. Steam practically shoots from her ears. "*Bride of Slug Man*? Where did that come from?"

"I thought it up last night," I mumble. "I know it sounds a little weird, but it's going to be fun. I found a great costume on the Internet. And there's going to be tons of romance. . . ."

Alyssa rolls her eyes. "I do not want a romantic scene with someone in a slug costume. Can't we find a better idea?"

If only Tristan hadn't asked about my movie in front of everyone and put me on the spot. I would have told Alyssa first in private. Then I could have ditched the idea and returned the costume when I found out how much she hated it. Now, if I junk *Bride of Slug Man*, it will be like admitting my idea is a dud compared to Tristan's. So far today, we've determined that I haven't won any cool film awards, I have no idea what French New Wave cinema is, *and* I come up with lame ideas.

"Wait until I finish writing it," I tell Alyssa. "You'll see. It's going to be amazing."

I'm not sure if I'm trying to convince Alyssa or myself. As we hurry to class, the scene with Tristan replays in my mind. "Hey, don't you think it's weird that, you know, nobody said anything to Margaret that whole time?" I'm hurrying to keep up with Alyssa's long stride. "Everyone just ignored her."

Alyssa shrugs. "It sucks, but it's always been that way for Margaret. You can't change people."

She sounds so nonchalant. It bothers me because I suspect Alyssa only hangs out with Margaret because of me. At lunch, sometimes I catch her eyes drifting over toward Lydia's table. Alyssa and I have been best friends since first grade, but she and Lydia became buddies during our fight. Before we started sitting with Margaret and Doris, they were chilling somewhere near Antarctica on the social map at school. What if Alyssa feels like she's sitting at the loser table? What if she's a social snob? I don't want to have to choose between my friends.

I cast a sideways glance at Alyssa. "Maybe we should have introduced Margaret to Tristan."

She expels a lungful of air. "I didn't think about it. I was too busy listening to your wacko movie idea."

Remembering how Paul treated me, I finally decide I did Margaret a favor by staying quiet. Alyssa's right—I can't change people's behavior all by myself.

"I'll show you the first scene at lunch," I promise Alyssa. "You're going to love it. We'll have great costumes and special effects. It'll be way more exciting than Tristan's movie. We're going to win that student prize at the film festival."

"You really think so?"

"Absolutely."

Suddenly, I want that prize more than I've ever wanted anything in my whole life. I need to win it. I have to prove to my classmates that I'm not Crapkate. I'm Medford Junior High's star filmmaker. And I'll show Tristan, too. The best way to fight a know-it-all is to beat him at his own game. If he's smart, I'll be smarter. If he knows about movie directors, I'll know more. If he drops film lingo into conversations, I'll memorize the whole dictionary. The film wars are on.

Luckily, I have the perfect resource. For Christmas, my parents gave me a book called *Let's Make a Movie!* It's stuffed with funny stories about how certain words came to be used by the movie industry. All I have to do is dig through the huge mess in my bedroom and find it when I get home.

At lunch, I survey the contents of the bag I packed for

myself. A sandwich, grapes, baked veggie straws, organic apple juice. Yawn. Just once, I wish my mother would buy bags of greasy potato chips for the days I take a lunch. I pop a grape into my mouth, suddenly feeling nervous. What if I show everyone the first pages of my script and nobody likes it? What if I turn into one of those Hollywood directors who make huge, expensive movies that bomb at the box office? I must be speed-biting my nails because Margaret suddenly grabs my hand. "You can pick up lots of germs from your fingernails," she informs me. "Why are you so jumpy?"

I take a deep breath and am about to pass out copies of my first scene when Paul bumps into Margaret from behind, just as she's taking a swig from a Cherry Berry juice. The red juice splashes all over her face and spills into her lap.

"Oops!" he calls with a grin over his shoulder. He and Blake laugh.

"Jerks!" Lizzy calls after them.

I search for Lunch Lady but she's on the other side of the room. The lunch mothers are all in a corner, gossiping. Typical. There's never a cop around when you need one.

I hand Margaret a napkin so she can wipe her face. "Something needs to be done about those two Neanderthals."

"I wish there *were* something we could do," Margaret mumbles. She keeps her head down, brushing over and over at the stain, even though it's clearly not coming out.

Poor Margaret. Some days it's hard to imagine being her. Lizzy hands her water and she wets the area, but it's no use.

"Your parents should send Paul's mother a cleaning bill," I say, trying to make her feel better. Margaret just sighs and keeps dabbing.

"What was your big announcement?" Doris asks.

I drag my eyes away from the bright red stain on Margaret's shirt. "Oh, yeah. Well, I decided what my next movie's going to be about."

That gets everyone's attention, except Alyssa. She makes a face at her sandwich. Clearly, the idea of a romantic Martian slug hasn't won her over yet.

"The next winner of the Big Picture Film Festival Young Filmmaker award is going to be . . ." I pause dramatically. I wish I had a drumroll app on my cell phone. ". . . a sci-fi romance called *Bride of Slug Man*!"

I hold up copies of the first scene with a flourish. Nobody reaches out to grab one. No one says anything at all. They exchange looks. My fragile self-esteem wilts like the lettuce from my failed salad. Nobody likes Slug Man except Derek. That should have been my first clue that it was a bad idea.

"Bride of Slug Man?" Lizzy repeats. "I thought it was going to be about werewolves."

Alyssa swallows a bite of sandwich. "It was supposed to be a romance."

"A musical romance," Margaret reminds her.

"Musical romances are corny," Alyssa snipes.

"How is *Sound of Music* corny?" Margaret flares. "Or *West Side Story*?"

This is not going the way I pictured it.

"A gastropod?" Doris asks. She points a dill pickle at me. "Did you know there are millions of different kinds of slugs? And that slugs, clams, and octopi are all considered mollusks? Did you know an octopus has three hearts? And if it loses a leg, it can grow it back."

Octopi? My head is spinning from Doris's sudden information overload. "That's amazing," I tell her. Creepy might be a better word.

Doris leans forward, still determined to wow me. "Did you know an octopus can squeeze through a hole no bigger than its eyeball? Think about that."

The thought of a squashed-up octopus trying to fit through its own eyeball is not appealing. I once went to a haunted house party where we were blindfolded and given cold eyeballs to hold, which turned out to be peeled grapes. I stare at the grapes I'm eating. My stomach lurches like I swallowed a cold tentacle that's now trying to regrow itself inside me.

"This isn't an octopus," I mumble. "It's half slug, half man. And it comes from Mars."

Margaret blinks. Alyssa sighs. Nobody looks impressed.

"A singing slug?" Margaret looks worried. "Is that what you mean?"

"Oh, yes," Alyssa says. "A romantic, singing slug. I can see it now. This is going to sweep the Oscars."

Alyssa has a problem with sarcasm sometimes. I decide to ignore her.

"No werewolves?" Lizzy asks wistfully.

"Maybe next time. But there's going to be romance, and singing, and . . . science." Then I remember what I told Tristan in the hallway. My stomach starts to churn, but it's too late to take it back. "The first day of shooting is this Saturday," I say casually.

"Saturday?" Margaret squeals. "That's in four days."

"I know it's not much time, but we can do it. There are a lot of people who said they want to be in my next movie. I'm going to make a sign-up sheet after school and hang it up. That will give me a better idea of how many are going to show up." I don't tell them this, but I also figure if people sign up, it makes it more official. They'll be less likely to bail on me and go to Tristan's auditions instead. "Don't worry, you guys will all have parts," I assure them.

Margaret takes a copy of the script and starts reading it over. "Who's going to be Adrienne?"

Dang. I wanted to avoid talking about who's going to be the star. I want Alyssa to play Adrienne, but what if Margaret or Lizzy wants the part? Will they be mad at me? How can I make it fair and still make sure Alyssa gets the part?

"I'd rather be in charge of props and wardrobe, and do

hair," Lizzy pipes up, as if she's reading my mind. "I don't really like acting."

I breathe a sigh of relief. "Sure, that would be great. I'm going to need a lot of help."

I glance sideways at Alyssa. Normally she would be acting all excited by now, but she doesn't say a word. She puts the flat end of a plastic knife on top of a stray grape and then pounds it with her fist. Squishy grape innards fly everywhere. A purple shred lands on Margaret's wrist. She frowns and brushes it off, then flicks it back at Alyssa. Alyssa narrows her eyes.

Hmmm. I know, it doesn't sound like much, but it could be huge. Seventh-grade girls are like sailors. We sniff the wind, watch for signs, trying to figure out which way the social wind is blowing. It's a well-known fact that the rules of middle-school friendship are way too complicated for the average adult mind. What if this is a case of pretend friend syndrome? Pretend friending is when two girls have a common friend. They both want to hang out with her so they act like they're pals, even when they don't really like each other. Is this what's going on between Alyssa and Margaret? I hope not. I've seen pretend friend dramas and it's not pretty.

I shouldn't assume the worst. Maybe Alyssa's just mad because she wants a movie script with romance, not alien ooze. I just need to show her that a great movie can have both.

"There are lots of parts," I say diplomatically, handing

everyone else a script. "And this is just the first scene. The second scene is going to be a big wedding. Adrienne will be in a gorgeous wedding gown. . . ."

Alyssa glances up. Suddenly, I have her attention.

"The handsome groom will be in a nice suit—"

"A tux," Alyssa interrupts.

"Fine, a tux. And every wedding has someone who sings a song, right? So that will be you, Margaret."

Margaret gives me a big grin. I breathe a sigh of relief. Now, Alyssa can play Adrienne and Margaret won't mind.

"It will be a beautiful wedding, with tons of guests and flowers. And scientists," I add, glancing at Doris. "Because the groom is a scientist, and all his coworkers are there. Anyway, after they say 'I do,' the groom will kiss the bride. . . ."

Alyssa plays it cool but a tiny smile plays around her mouth. "And then what? What happens after that?"

I scratch my nose. "Uh, well, then Slug Man breaks in, spews toxic slime, and turns the groom into an alien like him."

"Wow, it's kind of symbolic, isn't it?" Margaret says. "You know, the animal within. Reason versus rage. Brain versus instinct."

We all stare at her. Margaret is like a miniature English professor. She actually likes to read old classics by dead authors. We all watched the movie musical *Les Miserables*. Margaret read the book.

"So, who are you thinking for the groom?" Lizzy asks.

"Well, I was hoping Jake Knowles would do it," I say casually. "What do you think?"

Lizzy grins. "I think I changed my mind. Can I be Adrienne?"

We all laugh. Jake is a CAN guy—Cute, Athletic, and Nice. Like, CAN make girls melt. CAN crack funny jokes and CAN shove deserving people against lockers (boys love that kind of stuff). All the teachers like him because he's smart. I'd probably have a crush on him too, except Alyssa got there first. Most boys only rate two out of three on the CAN scale, or even one out of three. Paul Corbett is a big fat zero for three.

"I guess Jake's as good as anyone." Alyssa throws me a *you're-the-best-friend-ever* smile and then bites into a cookie with gusto. If I don't make it as a Hollywood director, maybe I can get work as a matchmaker.

I glance over at the next table. Tristan is sitting on top of it, leaning back on one arm, feet kicked up on the seats, talking with a couple boys. We're not allowed to sit on the tables. Lunch Lady is standing with her back to him, almost like she's ignoring him on purpose. Has he hypnotized her, too? Everyone else follows my gaze.

"I heard Tristan is making a movie," Lizzy says.

"It's called *Belly of the Naked Beast*," Margaret tells her. "It's a crime drama." Is there a hint of envy in Margaret's voice?

"If you guys want to try out for Tristan's movie, that's

fine with me," I say quickly. "I don't want you to feel like you have to be in mine."

They'd better want to be in mine. What kind of friend jumps ship and joins the enemy just because he has a better movie script? Actually, that probably happens a lot in Hollywood. Maybe I should get used to the feeling.

"No way," Margaret says. "In fact, I'll help with your sign-up sheet if you want."

Still, Margaret can't help sneaking another peek at Tristan. One of the mom lunch ladies has finally caught up with him. He throws her a charming smile and slides down into a seat. A small sigh escapes me. Deep down, I think maybe even I would like to be in Tristan's movie.

After school, Margaret and I make a sign-up sheet and hang it in one of the main hallways. I like how my name looks in bright fluorescent marker—sort of official and important. Suddenly, we hear a sneering voice behind us.

"Oh, wow, Slug Man auditions. I can hardly wait."

It's who else but Paul and Blake, trolling the hallways, looking for trouble. Paul pulls out a fat black marker. "Where do I sign up, Crapkate?"

"Sorry, Paulie," I retort. "There aren't any parts for brainless fatheads."

"Wow, that is so funny!" Blake leans against a locker. "Almost as funny as Margorilla's face here." He jerks a finger at Margaret.

Paul smirks. "Kingsley was just telling us how stupid your movie sounds. He's like, have you ever heard of such a retarded idea? And I'm like, yeah, her name is Kate Walden."

At the mention of Tristan's name, my heart squeezes like it's been shrink-wrapped. He's trash-talking my movie behind my back?

"But that's okay," Paul goes on, "because I still want to sign up!" Before I can stop him, he draws a big fat *X* across the entire sign-up sheet.

"Paul!" Margaret grabs at his arm, which is pretty brave. Paul snatches her glasses, smears them all over with his fingers, and tosses them back to her, grinning. I guess he's noticed how Margaret likes her glasses really clean. Sure enough, she takes the spray bottle out of her backpack like she can't get his dirty fingerprints off fast enough. When Paul also tries to grab the mister, Margaret wheels around and sprays him right in the eye. Inwardly, I groan. Does she really think that's going to stop him? I wait for Paul to start laughing. Instead, he bellows like she plunged a dagger into his forehead. He grinds his palm into his eye and stumbles away toward the bathroom, swearing and threatening to annihilate us. Blake looks unsure of what to do without his fearless leader. Finally, he tears my sign-up sheet off the wall, throws it on the floor, and trails after Paul.

"Paul is such a potty mouth," Margaret says primly.

I break out laughing. "Margaret, what is in that bottle? I thought it was water."

"It's glass cleaner. I think it has ammonia." She peers after Paul. "I hope I didn't blind him."

"Are you kidding? That was awesome!"

Margaret bends down to pick up my sign. Her face is pink; I can tell she's still upset. I feel bad that I laughed. Blake may have torn down my poster, but Margaret always gets the worst of their name-calling and stupid jokes. "Sorry that, you know, they started picking on you. If you hadn't been here with me—"

Margaret tries to smooth the creases out of my sign, avoiding my gaze. "It doesn't matter where I am. It happens all the time."

I wince at her words. Still, what can be done about it? It's like we need Sal's Mafioso grandfather to come teach Paul and Blake some manners.

Margaret gives me a tired smile. "Come on, let's rehang your sign."

We cover up the worst of Paul's black *X* with some Wite-Out and rehang it. Still, it looks funny now—like some amateur, homemade sign-up sheet that nobody will want to put their name on.

The rest of the week goes by in a lightning-bolt blur as I try to get ready for my first shoot. I'm also busy studying movie lingo in *Let's Make a Movie!* I try to memorize ten new terms every day. I even give myself quizzes to make sure I remember them. Sooner or later, Tristan and I are destined for another showdown, and I want to be ready. It's also good training for my future Hollywood career. I learn that two-sided tape is called *snot tape* because when you roll it into a little ball, it looks like, well, you know. And a *shower curtain* is a large plastic sheet used to soften lighting. I'm so ready for Tinseltown. And Tristan.

On Wednesday, Lizzy, Alyssa, and I walk to the local thrift mart after school. We make a beeline to the rack of used wedding dresses. Alyssa loves trying on all the glittery gowns. A lot of them are too big; others are way too ugly. Finally, she sweeps out of the dressing room and strikes a pose.

Lizzy puts her hands to her mouth. "You look beautiful!"

Alyssa grins and fluffs the dress. It fits her like a glove. It's white, it's sequiny, it's gorgeous, and it only costs twenty dollars. "Perfect!" I exclaim. "You look amazing!" Who says sci-fi can't be romantic?

Lizzy fusses over the dress, picking off pieces of lint and telling me she'll fix a small rip. I'm not worried; the camera will never see it. Still, it's funny to see her so fired up, like she's planning an actual wedding.

"Look." Lizzy points to a nearby rack. "We can get a suit for Jake for only ten dollars!"

My inner producer gets super excited over the cheap price. I could save a lot of money! My inner director scoffs.

If this movie is going to be perfect, then the groom needs a tux. Besides, I told Alyssa I would rent one. "We do need a suit for Jake, but not for the wedding."

I explain my idea, which I stole from old reruns of *The Incredible Hulk*. We'll buy a cheap black suit so the color matches the tux. Then, we'll tear out some seams and sew them back loosely by hand. Lizzy can grab the fabric and pull hard on the loose stitches while I shoot a close-up of the seam ripping apart. With the costume showing through underneath, it will look as if Christopher the scientist is transforming into a huge, horrible slug man. After the close-ups, I'll cut back to a wide shot of the creature with shreds of suit hanging from him.

Lizzy goes crazy over the idea. We find a suit and she volunteers to fix the seams so it looks Hulk-esque. Alyssa picks out fake pink flowers for her bouquet, and I even find a couple slightly dirty lab coats in the costume section. When we're finished, I count out forty dollars for the cashier. My funds are shrinking fast. Still, it's all worth it. Every detail of my movie is going to be perfect.

Well, almost every detail. When I check my sign-up sheet on Friday, I can't believe it. Tristan has put his audition sign-up right next to mine. Out of all the places in the universe to hang it, he sticks it side by side with mine! He must be trying to sabotage my movie. The worst part is, it's working. My sign-up sheet is completely empty, except for eight names. Eight lonely scrawls, and three of them belong to Alyssa, Margaret, and Doris. Four others also wrote down their names but then crossed them off. That's odd. I check Tristan's board. Sure enough, the four all signed up on his sheet. Kendall Carlton and Grace Devlin are two that scratched off their names and went with Tristan. I'm friendly with both of them. We chat in class and they told me they wanted to be in my movie. What gives? It feels like a slap in the face, as if they've all unliked me. The rest of the empty lines stare accusingly at me. Out of an entire middle school, only eight people want to be in my movie.

I take a closer look at the kids who did sign up. Olivia Sykes's name is there, along with Nathaniel Morgan, Trevor Jackson, and two sixth graders. That's my cast, along with my friends. I know why Nathaniel signed up. He's liked Alyssa for forever, which is about the same amount of time that she has liked Jake. It seems like the biggest problem in middle school is that everybody likes the wrong person.

Lydia's name isn't there. Jack Timner and Scot Logan didn't sign up. Neither did Jake Knowles. What happened to all those kids who were bragging about me just a few days ago? They all signed up for Tristan's audition. Spineless, flip-flopping, wishy-washy traitors. Tristan's sheet already has twenty-five names. Across the top, it reads, *FOOD! PIZZA! SODA!*

He's using bribery! How pathetic. I can't believe I didn't think of that. It doesn't matter, though. Everyone obviously likes Tristan's movie idea way better than mine. Or maybe they just like him better. My eyes feel hot as I realize I'm not standing in front of two sign-up sheets. I'm standing in front of a popularity contest. It's me versus the new kid, and he's winning, big-time. It's so embarrassing. How can I compete with a cute, award-winning, know-it-all snob from the Big Apple?

Someone nudges me from behind. It's Alyssa. She nods at the boards. "People are stupid. They're just trying to impress Tristan."

I shrug. "They can do whatever they want. I don't care."

"Yeah," she agrees. "Who needs them?"

We both know that I *do* care, a lot, but I appreciate that Alyssa is pretending along with me. Suddenly, she stiffens. "Jake signed up for Tristan's movie."

"Yeah, I saw that." I sigh, knowing I've let Alyssa down. Does she think I'm a failure? Maybe she secretly wishes she could be in *Belly of the Naked Beast* with Jake. I need to convince him to be in my movie. It's the least I can do for my best friend. I'm just not sure how to do it. He's always surrounded by his buddies.

In History class, I stare at the back of Grace Devlin's head. Usually, she turns around to talk to me. Today, she faces forward, sitting ramrod straight, like her back might break in two if she tries to swivel. What's going on? Do I have bad breath or something? I guess there's only one way to find out. Mr. Eisley is writing names and dates on the chalkboard. I lean forward and tap Grace's shoulder. She turns and gives me a nervous smile. I get right to the point. No chitchat today. "Grace, why did you take your name off my sign-up sheet?"

Her smile trickles away. She glances at Mr. Eisley. "Paul Corbett," she whispers. "I'm sorry, Kate, but I don't want to be a target. You know how he is. And he told me I should sign up for Tristan's movie instead. He told Kendall to switch, too."

Mr. Eisley turns back to the class and Grace whips around. I'm stunned at the news. Paul is convincing people to sign up for Tristan's movie so they won't be in mine. But why would he care, unless Tristan put him up to it? Mr. Eisley's words blur in my ears. My eyes feel blurred, too. It's just so . . . mean. Tristan already has lots of people trying out for his movie, and it's still not enough. Boy, I heard New Yorkers were tough, but I didn't know they were cutthroat. I suddenly wish my mother were home. I wish I could ask her if boys in her school ever turned out to be completely different than what she thought. She might not have any solutions for me, but she's really good at making problems seem smaller. And right now, this problem with Paul and Tristan seems huge.

Mr. Eisley suddenly kicks the garbage can to wake us up. "And now it's time for a pop quiz on the Peloponnesian War! Get your pens out!"

I groan. Grace turns around and rolls her eyes at me. Mr. Eisley hands out the sheets and the room goes quiet.

It's hard for me to focus, so I'm only halfway through mine when Jake stands up and hands in his quiz. I overhear him ask for a pass. Bathroom break. We're supposed to be old enough that we don't leave class to use the bathroom, but some teachers don't care. Mr. Eisley is in the "don't care" category. He's one of the fun teachers, always cracking jokes and throwing Ping-Pong balls if we're not paying attention. Sometimes the boys fake being asleep just so they can get "pinged" by Mr. Eisley.

This is my chance. If I can get Jake to be in my movie, that would be huge. Paul wouldn't dare give him a hard time. I finish my quiz as fast as I can. As I hand it in, I tell Mr. Eisley I also need a pass.

"You too, Walden? You're not running off with Knowles are you?"

I laugh and, because it's Mr. Eisley, I say, "Too much chocolate milk at lunch."

"You can never drink too much chocolate milk." He hands me a pass, then slaps his big belly. "Or maybe you can."

The hall is deserted. I stop at the cooler and take a long drink, waiting for Jake. After I've drunk so much water that I really do have to go to the bathroom, he finally shows up. We do a casual "hey" at each other as he heads back to class. I walk two steps to the bathroom, take a deep breath, and turn.

"Oh, Jake, remember you asked once about my next movie? Do you still want to be in it?"

He looks embarrassed, which means he doesn't. Now I'm embarrassed, too. What was I thinking, running after him?

"I'd like to, but I told Tristan I'd try out for his movie. You know, to be a gangster."

"Oh, sure." I stare at my feet, thinking furiously. And then it hits me—who says Jake can't be in two movies? "There's a part in mine I think you'd be perfect for," I blurt. "And you'd only have to be in a few scenes. So you could still be in Tristan's movie, too."

My heart is thudding. What if he says no? I can't beg; that would be too humiliating.

Jake hooks his hands in his back pockets, thinking. "What's the part?"

"You're a scientist and you're getting married. It's your wedding day. After that you, uh, you turn into a monster, so anyone can play that part. It doesn't have to be you."

I can feel myself blushing. It's feeling weirder by the minute, the two of us standing alone in the empty hallway. Is this what Hollywood directors have to go through to sign a star?

Jake grins. "Who's the bride?"

Of course he wants to know that. I try to sound casual. "Alyssa Jensen." I watch him like a hawk for telltale signs of interest.

"Oh, yeah," he says vaguely. "She was in your last movie, wasn't she?"

Okay, that didn't sound like tons of enthusiasm. I'll leave

that part out when I tell Alyssa. "Yeah. She's really good." I want to add *and she's really pretty and really fun*, but that might sound a little creepy.

Jake shrugs. "Sure, I guess I could do that, if it's just one day. Let me know when, okay?"

"It's tomorrow. I know that's the same day as Tristan's auditions, but we'll finish early so you can still go."

Jake flashes me his CAN smile. "That's okay. Tristan said he definitely wants me in his movie. I don't really have to try out."

Of course he wants Jake in his movie. Who wouldn't?

"That's great! Thanks, Jake!" I'm so happy that I almost walk back to class with him. I catch myself just in time and hurry off to the bathroom, where I do a fist pump. Alyssa will be thrilled. I'm happy too, because I have the perfect groom for my movie. Even Paul can't ruin that.

My good mood stays until passing period, when I see Nathaniel and Trevor by my sign-up sheet, crossing off their names. I hurry over. "Hey guys!"

Nathaniel jumps at my voice. "We're taking off our names but we're still going to be in your movie," he says in a low voice, glancing around.

I cross my arms. "Did Paul tell you to do this?"

Nathaniel's face turns red. "Paul thinks we should try out for Tristan's movie. But we want to be in yours. So, just don't tell, okay?"

Trevor looks glum. He's probably worried that Paul will

find out. This must have been Nathaniel's idea so he can be near Alyssa. "I won't say a thing," I promise.

After they leave, I tear down my sheet. It's too embarrassing to leave it hanging. I guess this will make Tristan happy. He can smirk to himself and feel superior. Well, maybe he's won the popularity contest, but we'll see who's laughing when I walk off with the festival prize.

Finally, Saturday morning arrives. The big day. April weather in the Midwest is a toss-up. It can be balmy and beautiful, or it can blizzard. When I peek through my curtains, the sun is shining. I open my window. The birds sound like an orchestra warming up for a dazzling performance. The sun is a yellow butterball melting over the trees and fields. I take a deep breath of pure country air.

Big mistake. I clutch my throat, coughing, and slam shut the window. Usually, the cow farm down the road is downwind of us, but the wind has shifted. The warmer weather must have thawed things over at Mr. Cunningham's place because the air reeks of cow manure. My entire cast of nine people, including Jake, is coming to my house today for the big wedding scene. And now the air smells and everyone will probably make jokes about cow poop, which will remind them about my old nickname. What will Jake think? I sink to the floor, feeling dizzy. Of all days, why did the wind have to shift today?

All I can do is add it to my long list of things I'm pretending not to care about. Anyway, it's still two hours before anyone shows up. Maybe the wind will change again. As I get dressed, the tux I rented for Jake catches my eye. It's hanging on my closet door, shiny and new looking. Yesterday, my dad and I swung by Armando's Formalwear to pick it up after school.

"Wow," he said to me, "this is a fancy production."

My heart lifts as I touch the rich black fabric. I was lucky that Doris's aunt works for Armando's because she got me a huge discount. Still, I used almost all the rest of my money to pay for it. Right beside the tux is the box with my new slug costume, which arrived in the mail yesterday. The costume is perfect—creepy and scary and sluggy. My cell phone rings and I run to grab it, full of dread. Why would anyone be calling at this hour, except to cancel? It's only my mother, though. I clutch the phone to my ear, happy to hear her voice.

"Just calling to wish you good luck with everything today," she says cheerily, "and to see how you're all doing."

"Thanks. We're fine. Dad is feeding the hens right now. He said he'd do it since I've got my shoot today. How's all your chicken stuff going?"

"Going great. I've learned a lot. I'll tell you all about it when I get home."

"You're coming today, right?"

My mother hesitates. "Your grandmother's cold turned into bronchitis. I'm thinking maybe I should go back and stay with her a few more days after the conference. What do you think? Can you and Derek handle the hens a little while longer?"

I make a face at myself in my mirror. The hens are the last thing I want to worry about right now. Still, Grandma's sick. That can't be good at her age. I stick my tongue out at myself.

"Kate?"

"Uh, yeah, that's fine, you should stay with Grandma. We'll be fine here."

"Everything else okay?"

As I think about Paul and Tristan, it feels like a forty-pound sack of chicken feed is sitting on top of my stomach. Trying to explain it long distance seems too complicated, though. I can hear a loudspeaker blaring in the background over the phone, something about an omelet demonstration. Knowing my mother, she'll want to check that out. "Yep, everything's great. Say hi to Grandma." Just then, the doorbell rings downstairs. "Gotta go, Mom. Bye."

It's Alyssa, Lizzy, Margaret, and Doris. Their mothers wisely decided to carpool. They hurry inside, pinching their noses.

"Wow," Margaret says. "What is that smell?"

Lizzy hands me the altered Hulk suit. "Yeah, what happened to fresh country air?"

I guess the wind hasn't changed direction yet. "It's wet cow dung." I grin at them. "It doesn't get any fresher than that."

I give Alyssa her dress. She strokes the fabric and smiles at me. "This should be a fun scene."

"Are you kidding?" Lizzy cries. "You get to kiss Jake Knowles! Of course it's going to be fun! I love weddings!"

Alyssa turns pink and we all laugh. It makes us all a little breathless and nervous to joke about kissing boys. In fact, just the thought of it makes my stomach do a funny wiggle. Still, it's great they're all in such a happy mood. I send Alyssa into the bathroom to change. A few minutes later, she sweeps into the room and twirls around. We all *ooh* and *ahh* as she beams.

"Just think," I tell her. "If you lived in the old days, this really could be your wedding day."

"Yeah, they used to marry off young girls to fifty-year-old guys all the time," Lizzy pipes up.

"That's older than my dad," Margaret cries.

"In some parts of the world, they still make twelve-year-old girls marry old men," Doris points out. "They're like grandfathers, with long, gray beards."

Alyssa wrinkles her nose. "What a bunch of dirty old men. They should be ashamed of themselves."

We all gag and groan to show just how disgusting the thought is. My cell phone rings so I duck into the TV room because there's still a lot of gagging going on.

"Kate?" The voice is low and creaky, barely above a whisper. It sounds like a half-dead zombie victim. It also sounds a tiny bit like Jake Knowles. A bad feeling creeps into my stomach.

"Jake, is that you?"

"Yeah. I came down with a bad cold. I feel like a truck hit me. I'm really sorry but I won't be able to make it today."

"Oh, no," I groan. "Are you sure?"

"Sorry." He breaks into a loud wheezing cough. It sounds like he's hacking up a lung. "Can you maybe reschedule?"

"That's okay," I tell him. "Don't worry, I'll figure something out. I hope you get better soon."

After we hang up I feel nauseous, like I caught something from him over the phone. I need more time to think, but the others have followed me into the TV room.

"What's the matter?" Alyssa asks as soon as she sees my face. "Who was that?"

"It was Jake." I sink into a chair. "He caught a bad cold and he can't make it."

"No way!" Lizzy shouts. "He can't do that!"

"Is he really sick?" Alyssa's voice is suspicious. "I bet he's just faking." She's probably worried that Jake doesn't want to do the wedding scene with her.

"He's definitely sick. He sounded near death."

"I don't believe it," Alyssa groans. "After all this work. Now we'll have to reschedule."

The hugeness of this problem is starting to worm its way into my brain. "There's no time to reschedule. We're barely going to finish in time for the festival deadline as it is."

Alyssa's face looks almost as white as her dress. "There's no groom! Who am I supposed to marry?"

"Think fast," Lizzy says. "Who do we know that's more or less Jake's size who might be willing to do it?"

Alyssa crosses her arms and wheels on me. "We don't need anyone else! Jake already said he would do it! Can't we just shoot one day after school this week?"

My brain feels paralyzed. I can feel Alyssa's eyes boring into me. Should I postpone to keep her happy? I'll need most of a day to shoot the scenes with Jake. By next weekend, he'll be busy with Tristan's movie. Even if I do postpone, he probably won't be available.

"I've already rented the tux," I tell Alyssa. "I can't afford to rent it for another day. And everyone else is already on their way here. I'm sorry, but we have to shoot today."

"And if Kate postpones, it's not fair to everyone else," Margaret chimes in. "We're already here, and the others will be here in a few minutes."

I know Margaret is just trying to help, but it's like she's drawing an invisible line. I either do what's best for Alyssa, or I do what's best for my other friends. I feel like I'm the rope in a game of tug-of-war. Whichever direction I go, a friend gets left in the lurch. Alyssa's chin quivers as she stares from Margaret to me.

"Fine," she snaps. "I don't even care!" She storms out of the room and slams the bathroom door shut.

I collapse in a chair. What do big-time directors do when a star gets ill? They probably shrug their shoulders and tack another million dollars on to the budget. I can't do that. I'm out of cash and out of ideas. Our house smells like cow poop, my leading man just tanked, and my star actress has locked herself in the bathroom. I almost wish I was working with my mother's hens again. At least they didn't call in sick. My big, inspirational first day is turning into a flop.

Worst of all, I've let Alyssa down. She got splattered with buckets of blood while filming *Night of the Zombie Chickens* and never complained. Well, hardly ever. Now, she wants a simple romantic scene with a certain somebody and I can't even manage it. I need to talk to her but I'm not sure what to say. Maybe I *should* just wait and shoot another day.

Margaret picks a sequin off the floor that fell from the dress. "She shouldn't blame you. It's not your fault Jake is sick."

I sigh and rake my hands through my hair. Margaret's right. Still, I may have to reschedule, whether I want to or not. "We don't have anyone to play Jake's part," I point out.

Doris is doodling on a notepad, scratching out hieroglyphics, which I assume are math symbols. "I know someone who might work." She writes on the pad and holds it up. *Noah Fleming.*

Lizzy hoots. "Nose Phlegmy?"

Doris frowns at her. "That's a stupid nickname."

I bite back a groan. Noah Fleming, the biggest science geek nerd at Medford Junior High? Still, he is about Jake's height, and he's not bad looking. I'm so desperate that I tell myself Doris is right. Maybe Noah could work. "Do you think he would do it?"

Doris settles the question by calling Noah. He's available. He doesn't mind marrying Alyssa. He can be here in half an hour.

All that's left is to tell the happy bride. Alyssa looks beyond horrified, as if she's woken up to find her face covered with zits and a huge, nasty cold sore sprouting on her lip. "I am not doing the wedding scene with Noah Fleming! No way. Forget it!" She starts ripping off the dress to show she means it.

"Alyssa." I try to stay calm but all the hysteria is getting to me. "Just think about it. You're the star. You have to do the wedding scene. I know it sucks that Jake is sick, but we have to move forward." My voice is a rising tide of panic. "We all have to be flexible! I've got more people showing up in fifteen minutes!"

Alyssa has been furiously tugging at the zipper, but now she quiets and heaves a big sigh. "The thing is, I don't even want to be Adrienne. I hate gooey stuff and I'm tired of getting splattered with blood and slime and gunk. I thought it would be fun to be in a scene with Jake just because, you know, he's a nice guy." She blushes as we all exchange knowing glances. "But if he's not going to be in it, then I'd really like to do something different this time."

"But the dress fits you!" I tell her. "Who else is going to do it?"

Alyssa bites her lip, then turns to Lizzy. "Can't you hem the dress? You know, just use tape or something?"

Lizzy shrugs. "I guess so. It shouldn't be too hard."

"Perfect. Lizzy can be Adrienne!"

We all gaze at tiny, petite Lizzy. Standing near Alyssa, she looks like a fragile moth next to a long-legged dragonfly. Even with a lot of hemming, it's clear the dress will never fit her.

"I'm too short," Lizzy says, which is nice because then I don't have to say it. "Maybe Margaret can do it."

Margaret shakes her head. "I'm singing a song at the wedding, remember? And . . . sorry Kate, but I really don't want to get slime on me."

Margaret carries lens cleaner and hand sanitizer in her backpack. Even I know she's not the best candidate to play Slug Man's love interest.

Doris rolls her eyes. "It's just condensed milk and cornstarch, right Kate? It's not like it's real slime. It washes out."

Alyssa finishes unzipping the dress and steps out of it. She holds it out to Doris. "Fine. Then you be Adrienne."

Doris doesn't laugh like it's a funny idea. She doesn't shake her head or make a face. No one else does, either.

"Sure!" Margaret cries. "Doris could do it!"

Everyone looks relieved that we've found a live body to plug into the dress. Except me. Doris is a great friend but she's not what I call a gifted actress. She was the head zombie in my last movie and the part fit her perfectly. Suddenly, everybody is looking at me. Should I insist that Alyssa do it? She'll be crabby for the whole production. And if I try to find someone else, won't I hurt Doris's feelings? Still, I'm the director. Sometimes hurt feelings can't be avoided.

"I can do it if you want, but I probably won't be very good," Doris says modestly.

"You'll be great!" Margaret cries.

Wonderful, supportive Margaret always tries to encourage everyone. She would make a lousy director.

"Doris, you were so good in *Night of the Zombie Chickens*," Alyssa chimes in. She turns to me. "Doris would be perfect!"

Alyssa blinks at me with her big blue eyes, trying to sell the idea. But she knows that I know that she knows that Doris would not be perfect. Alyssa is just trying to get out of doing it herself. I need to shoot down the idea right now. I have to be strong. I have to be directorial. That means forcing Alyssa to play the part. It also means embarrassing Doris, because nobody likes to be rejected in front of her friends. What if Doris is secretly thrilled at the idea of playing Adrienne? Right now she's polishing her glasses. If it were anyone else, I'd say it was an act to hide her excitement. With Doris, it's hard to tell. Maybe her glasses are just dirty.

Any decent director knows that you have to put your film in front of your friendships. Art before all. That's just the way it has to be. I stand up. My legs feel heavy; my stomach lurches. Everyone waits to hear my verdict.

"Sure!" I say. "Doris will be great!"

Doris's lip curls up in a smile. I give her a thumbs-up, inwardly groaning. What have I done? Tristan has his pick of girls for his leading lady. I've got Doris. Tristan has guns and gangsters. I have a slug man. I can already see his gloating expression as he waves the student award in my face. Everyone will carry him off on their shoulders, ticker tape and balloons raining from the sky as the school band grinds out an off-key victory march. I will be left in the dust, with bits of dirty confetti sticking to my shoe like dried chicken poop.

Suddenly, I've lost both my star actors. Cute, athletic, nice Jake Knowles has been replaced by nuclear nerd Noah Fleming. Pretty, blond-haired ace screamer Alyssa Jensen has bowed out. Bespectacled Doris, who lives in bulky brown sweaters and sweatpants, who shows excitement by raising an eyebrow, is my new romantic heroine.

I know I should have said something, but how could I? Maybe film trumps friendship in Hollywood, but not in seventh grade. Everyone might have gotten mad at me.

Suddenly, Lizzy squeals: "We need to get Doris ready!"

Doris gets swept upstairs in a tornado of girl energy. Once they're gone, I cover my face with my hands. How many more things can go wrong before we even get started? I hear happy shrieks and the sound of ripping duct tape.

As Doris squeezes into the dress upstairs, my phone rings. Maybe it's Jake! Maybe he's feeling better! It's not too late to turn this thing around!

"Hi, Kate, it's Tristan."

My blood freezes, and so does my brain. Tristan Kingsley is calling me? The guy who ruined my movie is calling on my first day of shooting? It's a bad omen. How did he get my phone number? Then I remember—Lydia has it. Some of the other kids probably do, too. I realize I haven't said anything and the silence is stretching out. "Uh, hi."

"I just wanted to see how your shoot's going. I know how crazy first days get."

It's only ten in the morning! Does he think we started at the crack of dawn? I haven't shot a single scene yet. Dread clutches at me. It's like he's implying that I'm already running behind. And the silence is stretching out again.

"Uh, fine."

I can hear a noisy hum of voices in the background behind him. Suddenly, a girl screams. Lydia. I roll my eyes. Now I get it. He's calling to show off. All my schoolmates are there at his auditions, and he wants to rub it in. He probably told them to talk extra loud so I'd be sure to hear it.

"I'm just starting auditions," he says carelessly. "What a mess. So, how are things going?"

Wow, this guy is nosy. "It's going amazing. Fantastic. This has been the absolute perfect first day of shooting so far. No problems whatsoever."

Okay, I'm laying it on a bit thick, but he's got a lot of nerve, calling and checking up on me. The babbling voices behind him break into squeals of laughter. It sounds like a big party. I feel a wobble of sadness in the pit of my stomach. If I wasn't busy making my own movie, I could have been in his. I guess his phone call worked, because now I really feel low. I'm glad when the doorbell rings. It gives me an excuse to get off the phone.

"I've gotta go," I blurt. "Someone's here."

"Okay, see you later."

Not if I can help it. I'm staying as far away from Tristan Kingsley as possible. I run to the door.

It's Noah.

"Smells like bovine methane," he informs me as soon as he steps inside. He's grinning nervously, his eyes darting around the kitchen. Maybe I'm supposed to laugh because he adds, "That's cow gas."

"Yeah, ha-ha, I know." I hand him the tux and point him toward the bathroom.

As soon as he disappears, a stampede thunders down the stairs and Doris's stylists pull her into the kitchen. They've removed her glasses and blow-dried her hair into a soft wave. With makeup and a little lipstick, and in the long, sequined white dress, she looks like a different person.

"Doris, you look great!" I exclaim.

She also looks nervous, like a fish out of water. Way out, like stuck on a cactus in the desert somewhere. She pulls at the dress and tugs at her hair until Lizzy slaps her hands away.

"You're a bride! Stop fidgeting."

The dress is a little snug but it works. Lizzy did a good job hemming with the duct tape, if you don't look too closely. Doris has probably never worn anything this form-fitting in her life.

Noah comes in, tugging at the sleeves of the tux. He stops short and his Adam's apple bobs as he gulps. "Wow, Doris, is that you? You look . . . different."

Lizzy and Margaret giggle and Doris looks like she wants to bury her head in a book. "So, um, how did you do on the math test?" she finally asks.

Noah looks relieved. "One hundred four percent. You?"

"One hundred six."

Noah clutches his head as Doris smirks. "I can't believe I messed up," he groans.

Alyssa rolls her eyes. "Yeah, only slightly better than perfect, that's rough. How do you even get more than one hundred percent on a test?"

"Extra credit," Noah and Doris chime together.

"Of course," Alyssa mutters. She has a hard time with the regular problems, much less the extra credit.

Lizzy is already fussing with the tux. It hangs a bit loose but it's not too bad. All dressed up, Noah looks nice. You wouldn't know he was a super geek until he opens his mouth.

"Hey Doris, why did the chicken cross the Möbius strip?"

Doris's lip quirks. "Why?"

"To get to the same side."

Doris starts honking like a goose with a head cold. Noah's laughter pings around the room like he's hiccupping. He notices the rest of us aren't chuckling.

"A Möbius strip is a continuous surface with only one side," he informs us. Noah always talks really fast and kind of jerky, like he's got a caffeine drink running through his veins.

"It's formed from a long, narrow strip..." Doris interrupts him.

"...you rotate one end of the strip 180 degrees and tape it to the other end!" Noah finishes triumphantly. "If you have some paper I could show you."

Doris is way ahead of him. Before I can stop her, she grabs my dad's newspaper and rips a long strip off the front page. Messing with the newspaper before my dad has had his coffee is like poking a hungry bear with a sharp stick. You don't do it unless you like big, grumpy, and mad all rolled into one. Hopefully, we'll be outside before my dad discovers one third of the day's headlines are gone.

Doris gives the strip a half twist, then ducks down and rips a piece of tape off her dress. As she tapes the ends of the paper together, Noah tries to grab it from her.

"Here, let me," he says. "I can do it..."

Doris shoots him one of her I-just-ate-a-sour-pickle-so-don't-mess-with-me frowns. "I *know* how to do it."

This doesn't deter Noah. In fact, he finds it immensely funny. He's doing his hiccuppy laugh and saying *okay, okay, okay.* Any moment, I expect his head to shoot off and start bouncing around the walls. I feel like I need to down a double frappé just to keep up with him.

Doris holds up the strip of paper. "You see? It doesn't have two sides. It's just one continuous side."

The rest of us stare at the strip and trace it with our fingers. It *is* kind of cool. Still, these two have some kind of strange competition going on. Alyssa leans over and whispers to me, "This is going to be one weird wedding."

The doorbell rings again. It's the two sixth graders, Darcy and Rebecca. They're quickly followed by Nathaniel and Trevor and then Olivia. I assign Nathaniel to play the pastor. Trevor has two parts. First, he'll be a scientist guest at the wedding. Then, since he's the tallest, he'll later play Slug Man. Alyssa is now Shannon, the bridesmaid. The rest will be wedding guests. Derek wanders downstairs in his pajamas just then, rubbing his eyes.

"Your friends are noisy," he complains.

"We're shooting, Derek, remember? Don't you want to help?"

He yawns. "I guess so."

I need Derek's Super Soaker gun for the sliming during the wedding scene. He said I could only use it if I let him be in my movie. While Derek gets dressed, I move everyone outside. It still smells like bovine methane. Maybe it's just as well Jake didn't make the shoot. Everybody holds their noses and makes dumb jokes about gas. I try to divert their attention by showing them the wedding area, which I arranged the day before in our backyard. I hung pink streamers and balloons from the trees overhead and set out a few rows of chairs. In front, there's a table covered by a white cloth and some fake greenery. It looks festive, if I do say so myself.

I've decided to shoot Margaret's solo first. She whips out her iPod and plugs it into my portable system. The song blares through the tinny speakers. Perfect. I was kind of worried the music might slow the pace of my movie. Luckily, she picked a short song. Listening to her sing, I realize the pretty melody will add production value. It will look like the director is contrasting the purity of music against the beastlike horror of the slug man. Maybe I should write that down for the judges, just in case they miss it.

Doris's march down the aisle is next. I have to keep my shot tight because I barely have enough people for wedding guests, thanks to Tristan. Derek sits in the back row, in mismatched pants and shirt, mumbling into his spy watch. Olivia sits near him, popping her gum. I even make Lizzy take a seat next to Margaret so the audience will look bigger. We borrowed one of my mother's dresses for Alyssa, and Lizzy pinned it to make it fit her. Noah stands near Nathaniel, fingering the collar of his shirt like it's too tight. He looks nervous, but I guess that's how a groom should look. Nathaniel stands behind the table, facing the bride and groom. Everyone is in place. The big moment is at hand.

I take a deep breath. "Okay, action!"

Margaret starts the wedding march song on her iPod and the traditional chords ring out through the speakers. Alyssa starts forward, smiling, followed by Doris. She trudges down the aisle like she's still in sneakers and sweatpants. Okay, maybe it's not perfect, but she does look pretty carrying the pink bouquet of flowers. Now it's time for the vows.

"Okay, take Doris's hand," I tell Noah, "and look into her eyes."

Suddenly, the boy looks like he's about to melt into a puddle on the ground. He tugs at his tie as if it's choking him, then shyly takes Doris's hand. Doris is staring at her shoes like she just stepped in something awful.

"Doris, you have to look at him," I bark. "And smile! It's not a funeral!"

Finally, Doris lifts her eyes to meet Noah's. Her entire face turns bright pink, but that's nothing compared to her ears. They turn so red it looks like third-degree sunburn. That's when it *finally* sinks into my thick skull.

Doris and Noah like each other.

That's why he's acting so nervous and jumpy. That's why she's laughing at everything he says. Duh. It's so obvious, I can't believe it took me this long to figure it out.

I glance over at Alyssa. She bites her lip to keep from grinning. We both have to squash a desire to go *Awwwww*. Who knew that shy, genius Doris had a crush? She can pretend otherwise but the neon ears are a dead giveaway. The best part is, they don't have to act. They smile dopily at one another as they run through their vows, just like a real bride and groom.

Nathaniel keeps looking at Alyssa, even though he's supposed to be focusing on the happy couple. "Christopher," he intones. "Do you take this woman to be your bride?"

"I do," Noah squeaks.

"Adrienne, do you take this man to be your husband?"

"I do."

Nathaniel licks his lips, which look painfully chapped, and shoots another glance at Alyssa. "I now pronounce you man and wife! You may kiss the bride!"

I do a double take. I never told Nathaniel to say the kissing part! He smirks at Alyssa. For a pastor, he's a little creepy. What will Noah do? He looks frozen in place, except for his Adam's apple, which is working overtime. Finally, he slowly leans toward Doris. He's going to kiss her! We all hold our breath. Uh-oh. Doris is starting to frown. Noah's head stops, swaying back and forth like a bobblehead. Finally, he whispers, "Doris, did you know a cat has nine tails?"

Wha-a-at? I'm pretty sure that's not in the script.

Doris wrinkles her nose. "Huh?"

"Here's the proof. No cat has eight tails. A cat has one tail more than no cat. Therefore, a cat has nine tails." Noah rattles this off at top speed. He giggles as Doris honks.

Alyssa is biting her lip, trying not to laugh. I sigh. I guess we'll just skip the kiss. Doris's ears might ignite if any more blood rushes into them.

"Cut!" I shout.

At least the wedding went better than I expected. Alyssa hurries over. Any sadness she felt at missing her big scene with Jake is long gone.

"Can you believe it?" she whispers. "How did we not see this? They're so cute together!"

She turns and throws a huge smile at Doris and Noah. "Nice job you two! You make a great couple!"

Doris ducks her head and frowns. Noah smiles goofily.

"We've got to get them together!" Alyssa says, in a whisper loud enough to wake the dead.

"Well, right now we have to drag them apart," I tell her. "This is where Slug Man crashes the party."

Finally. We survived the wedding. It was a little tricky, but not nearly as complicated as the next scene. It's time for a little mayhem, and a lot of slime.

10

My dad must have sneaked out in the car while we were shooting, because he shows up with take-out pizzas. Just in time, because I'm starving. Everyone else must be too, because they all snatch up slices and the pizza is gone in minutes. While everyone else talks, I'm busy worrying about what comes next. This is the scene I've been sweating over. Slug Man slimes Noah's character, scientist Christopher Jones, which changes him into a slug, too. Lizzy and I have concocted a putrid green slime based on the recipe that Derek and I cooked up.

When Trevor puts on the slug man costume, everybody *oohs* and *ahhs* over it. He runs after the sixth-grade girls, making hissing noises. Thrilled, they scream and run away. I grab my camera and run through my notes.

"Okay," I call. "Let's shoot this!"

Everyone ignores me. Trevor is still chasing Darcy and Rebecca. The others are chowing down on the snacks I put out.

"Come on, people!" Margaret barks. "Places, please! We're burning daylight!"

Wow. I give her a thumbs-up and she grins at me. I'm not used to hearing Margaret sound so commanding, although she has the big voice for it. She may have found herself a new career as a big-time Hollywood producer. Either that or an army drill sergeant. Everyone stops what they're doing and takes their places.

I turn to Noah. "Okay, I want you to hold Doris's hand and smile for a few seconds because the pastor just pronounced you man and wife. Trevor, you're going to run in, push Noah away, and grab Doris. And Doris, you have to scream a lot."

Noah giggles nervously as we rehearse the scene. I have to remind him that he shouldn't be laughing while his bride is being attacked. Doris, on the other hand, is practicing her stone impersonation. "You have to scream more," I tell her. "Your brand-new husband is going to be changed into a horrible monster right in front of you."

When Doris opens her mouth, nothing comes out except a croaky squeal, like a wet kitten with a bad cold. Every time we practice it gets fainter until finally she just frowns at me. I rake my hand through my hair. "Okay, let's do something different. Try and—"

"Like this!" Margaret cries. She screams right next to us, loud enough to restart the heart of a zombie. I jump about a foot and the hairs on my neck do a weird, tingly thing. It even unnerves the chickens. I hear them cluck and screech in their pen.

Doris's sour pickle face comes back. "Was that really necessary?"

"I'm just showing you how to scream," Margaret explains.

"That's great." I rub my ear. "Maybe just don't scream so close next time."

I'm starting to sweat, even though it's a cool day. How can I win an award with Doris mumbling and Noah fumbling? I'm tempted to do a quick script change and turn everyone into zombies. At least then they don't have to act. I chomp on a pencil, thinking hard. Finally, I park Margaret off-camera near Doris. When Doris opens her mouth, Margaret screams. I just have to hope the judges won't be able to tell. As we set up to shoot the scene, I pull Noah aside.

"Remember, Noah, Doris is your new bride. Do you want her to see you looking embarrassed or acting brave? This is your chance to impress her. I mean, you know, it's Christopher's chance to impress Adrienne."

Even mentioning that he's pretend married to Doris makes Noah blush. His face brightens at the idea of impressing her, though, so maybe I triggered a lightbulb in his overwired brain.

It's finally time for the big slime scene. I speed-walk around the set, chewing on one fingernail after another, trying to remember what I'm forgetting. I can't think of anything, but I still can't bring myself to start shooting. Once somebody gets slimed, there's no redo because they're going to be a gooey mess. I'll have to hope for some one-take wonders. At first, I couldn't figure out how to show Slug Man shooting slime. My dad had the idea of hiding a tiny squirt gun inside one of the bulky gloves. Trevor can hold on to the gun and squirt it through a small hole we cut in the glove. The squirt gun has a puny stream, so when I'm showing the victims being slimed, I'll use Derek's Super Soaker off-camera. And that's how you spew slime on a small budget.

"Noah, after Trevor pushes you aside and grabs Doris, you're going to lift a chair, like you're about to throw it at him. Then, Trevor, you raise your hand and squirt him, okay? After that, I'll turn the camera around and get shots of Noah getting slimed."

"I get to shoot the Super Soaker!" Derek shouts right away. "It's my gun! I should get to do it!"

"Fine." I hand him the gun, loaded with slime. At least if something happens to it, he can't blame someone else for breaking it. I'm just hoping the slime doesn't clog the barrel. I made the batch extra liquidy, just in case.

"Now listen," I tell Noah. "We can't reshoot this because you're going to be a mess. So, no goofing up. No laughing. When the slime hits you, act like you're choking, and then shout and sink to the floor. You're mutating into a slug creature so you have to be really scared, okay?"

"Really scared. Got it."

"Places, everybody!" Margaret shouts. "Quiet on the set!"

At least she didn't shout it right in my ear. I take my place behind the camera. "Action!"

The first part goes fine. Trevor runs in, pushes Noah aside, and grabs Doris. As Noah raises a chair over his head, Trevor shoots a stream of slime at him with the squirt gun. Now for the big moment. I zoom in on Noah and cue Derek. He lets loose with the Super Soaker. Even I have a hard time not laughing when the first big gob of green slime hits Noah in the face. Derek doesn't stop when he's supposed to, though. Every time Noah opens his mouth to shout, Derek squirts him with a fresh flood. Pretty soon, he's coughing and gagging for real. Noah doesn't break out of character, though, I'll give him that. He holds up his arms to try and ward off the onslaught of ooze.

"Derek, that's enough!" I shout, but by then he's already emptied the gun. As Noah slips and slides in the pool of goo, he manages a hoarse, gurgling scream: "I've been sliiiiimed!" before collapsing to the ground.

"Cut!" Margaret shouts.

I turn to stare at her but she's hurrying to check on Noah. Now she's gone too far. Nobody cuts a scene except the director. I'm pretty sure that was the eleventh commandment God handed down to Moses—so important it was inscribed on its own stone tablet, which Moses left up on the mountaintop because he couldn't carry them all. One day someone will find it and this is what it will say: NOBODY SAYS CUT EXCEPT THE DIRECTOR. EVER. PERIOD.

I give Margaret a stern look, and try to make my voice sound commanding, like God thundering from the mountaintop. "Margaret, you cannot cut the scene. Only the director can do that."

"Sor-ry," Margaret mutters. "I'm just trying to help."

"You are helping. Just, maybe don't help so much."

When I first became friends with Margaret, she was so quiet. I can't believe that shy girl is now running around a movie set, screaming at the top of her lungs and shouting directions at everybody. I remember when she took a bow with Alyssa at my movie premiere, blushing as the audience cheered. Margaret has helped me out so much. It never occurred to me until now that maybe I've helped her, too. Which is a nice feeling, even if she is annoying me.

Doris is wiping the slime off Noah's face. "I almost drowned!" he tells her.

Doris snuffles. Encouraged, Noah takes it up a notch. "That stuff tastes nasty! I think I drank half a gallon!"

Alyssa and I grin at each other. It's so romantic. Still, the show must go on. I have a lot more shots to get.

"Okay, Noah, you need to clean off and get into the slug costume. Our next shot is when you transform."

After Noah has hosed off and suited up, I practically have to peel him away from Doris's side. He's busy reenacting some of his getting-slimed moves for her. I grab him by the elbow and drag him in front of the camera.

"Margaret has some lines here!" Lizzy calls, pointing to a battered script page.

I shoot her a grateful look. Lizzy is my script supervisor, helping me keep the scenes sorted out. This is the most complicated shoot I've ever done, with lots of people, props, and action. There's so much to remember, my head feels like a pressurized soda bottle, ready to shoot out in all directions. I show Margaret where to stand, then turn to Noah. "Can you fit your glasses on over the mask? I need you to wear those."

He fishes them out and puts them on. They hang crooked but they fit. Lizzy and I already got shots of the seams ripping on the thrift store suit, which I'll edit in later. Now, Noah puts on the shredded suit over the slug costume. It looks so perfect that a wave of excitement rolls over me. I'm making a movie! There's no biz like show biz! It feels like there's magic in the air around us—movie magic! I take in a deep breath and catch a whiff of a sharp, earthy odor, as if show biz even has its own special smell. Then I realize it's probably just Noah, sweating next to me in the slug man costume. I may need to put that thing through a wash cycle.

"Okay, Noah, the toxic slime has turned you into a Martian creature. When I cue you, slowly stand up. Margaret will say her lines. Then I want you to grab Doris and run off with her. Doris, you're scared now, so you're struggling."

Doris scratches her nose. "How can you have two slug men when you've only got one costume?"

Trust Doris to fret about the math. "The scientists in the wedding audience are going to capture the slug man from Mars and take him to their lab to study him," I explain. "Christopher is going to run off with Adrienne. So I only have to show one of them at a time. And Noah's slug creature wears glasses. That's how we'll tell them apart."

After I cue him, Noah slowly rises, glasses askew. Margaret, standing just behind him, screams, "He's one of them now! It's the slime that did it! Look out for the slime!"

Margaret is a good screamer, that's for sure. Even Doris does a good job struggling with Noah as he drags her away. "That was perfect!" I call. "Amazing!" I decide to keep pushing forward before I lose their attention. "In the next shot, Trevor plays the part of Sinclair, Christopher's scientist friend. Trevor, you're going to take a hypodermic needle out of your suit pocket and stick Slug Man with it. That knocks him out so you and Alyssa can drag him off to your lab. Noah, you can play Slug Man now since you're in the suit. So take off your glasses. Everyone got it?"

Trevor raises a hand like he's in class. "Why would I have a hypodermic needle in my pocket at a wedding?"

I clear my throat. "Good question. You and Alyssa are both scientists, so you always carry a hypodermic with you, just in case. It's sort of like how cops want to carry their guns even when they're off duty. You never know when you might need it."

Trevor looks confused but he doesn't argue. The real answer is that I wanted to make the story about Christopher and Adrienne. Having Slug Man change Christopher into a monster seemed the best way to combine romance, my cool slug costume, and flying saucers, all in one script. I know it's a stretch, but I've seen plenty of Hollywood movies with way bigger plot holes.

Lizzy hands Trevor the fake hypodermic needle, which she borrowed from her younger brother's Play Doctor toy set. Noah has loosened up since his slime performance and he puts on quite a show as Slug Man. After Trevor injects him with the fake hypodermic, he whips backward and falls among some chairs, then jerks up, careens toward the pastor's table, rolls across it, staggers drunkenly in the direction Doris went, spins twice, gurgles loudly, and collapses.

There's a moment of silence after Noah's spectacle, and then everyone breaks into peals of laughter. Noah turns red and grins as they clap. It turns out under that fumbling, geek-guy veneer there's a hard-core ham waiting for his chance in the spotlight. I just hope it all makes sense once I edit it together.

Suddenly, Nathaniel raises a hand. "Can I get slimed, too?"

All the boys want to be slimed. By the end, the wedding

set looks like a tornado hit it—chairs thrown everywhere, streamers ripped down, balloons popped, and gobs of goo dripping from the trees. I get a last shot of Trevor and Alyssa dragging away Slug Man and we're done for the day.

"Amazing job!" I tell everyone. "It looked fantastic!"

The entire cast and crew decide to jump into the pond to clean off, even though the water is really cold. Derek fills up his Super Soaker and blasts everybody. It's like a party. Everyone is splashing and screaming and having fun. I am, too, until I start worrying. Shooting chickens was so much easier, even if they did leave nasty surprises in the grass. I told everyone the scenes looked fantastic, but did they, really? I'm not sure. None of them went how I pictured them. In my daydreams, the scenes look like they're straight out of an epic Hollywood blockbuster, but reality is so much different. Maybe that's why my hopes of a perfect movie suddenly feel like they're trickling through my fingers like sand. The harder I try to grab hold, the more they seep away. Should I have done some shots differently? Were they too close up? Too wide? Did I make any mistakes? With every fresh worry, Tristan's face pops into my head. I can practically hear him laughing. And even though I know it's silly, I swear I can hear Steven Spielberg and George Lucas laughing with him.

On Monday morning it seems like everybody is talking about Tristan's auditions. Lydia charges into the bathroom while I'm in a stall and describes it for Sara Gonzalez, since she was out of town. "There were at least thirty people. He's got a mega TV screen and a pool table, and I ate way too much ice cream!"

Thirty kids tried out for Tristan's movie instead of mine. I try to wrap my head around this. I can't believe I ever thought I might like him even a tiny bit. I hate him almost as much as I hate Paul and Blake. My mother always tells me not to use the word *hate*, but what else should I call the black bitterness bubbling in my heart? Does that mean I'm a bad person? Is it okay as long as I don't call it hate? What's wrong with hate, anyway? My thoughts swirl around like the memories Harry Potter watches in Professor Dumbledore's Pensieve. I wonder if Harry got a headache, too, after a while.

It turns out that Tristan picked Lydia to be his mysterious high-society girl and Jack Timner will play his detective. Everyone else will play various gangsters and dames. I'm not even sure who I hear this from. The news seems to swirl in the air, passed from locker to locker, on everybody's lips. I wouldn't be surprised if they even broadcast it during morning announcements. I'm the only one who's *not* talking about it. When I spot Tristan headed my way in the hall, I pull a quick one-eighty and dive into the bathroom. Even though I've lived in Medford my whole life, it feels like he's moved in and pushed me aside. He convinced all my classmates to try out for his movie instead of mine. It feels like he stole something from me. He and Paul and Blake. That thing they stole—that happy feeling of knowing exactly where I fit and how I belong—well, I want it back.

As I hurry to class through the crowded hallway, keeping my head low, I notice Doris and Noah walking together, heading my way. Doris is speed-walking and doesn't slow down. I'm not even sure she sees me. As Noah gallops along beside her, I catch a sentence about some lab experiment gone horribly wrong. I smile to myself. It looks like Noah finally got the encouragement he needed. In fact, the bout of Extreme Ham Acting must have knocked something loose in his brain, because he's suddenly Mr. Social. At lunch, he plops down in the seat next to Doris and gives her a soppy grin. Margaret beams at them like they really did get married on Saturday. Doris seems to notice, because she shoots Margaret a huffy look. Still, we all agree later that Doris's romance is pretty adorable.

After school, Noah joins us again as we're hanging out near the buses, lifting up our faces to enjoy the sunshine.

"Hi, hi, hi." He nods rapid fire to everyone, then turns his goofy grin on Doris. "Hi Doris. Did you do the math assignment yet?"

Doris has just popped a vending machine cookie into her mouth. She shakes her head, chewing.

"I already did it. It's not too hard. I spent maybe half an hour, no, maybe twenty minutes on it, twenty-five, tops. Number thirteen was a little tricky. Don't worry, you won't have a problem." He rattles this off at top speed.

Doris swallows and looks at him. "What do you want?"

Noah's nervous laughter pings around us. "Nothing. Nothing, just wanted to see if, you know, you had a chance to . . ." His voice trails off.

"I haven't done it yet, okay?" There's an edge to Doris's voice.

Awkward silence.

"Noah, wasn't the shoot on Saturday fun?" Margaret chirps.

"Oh, yeah, yeah, that was great. That was fun." He

glances at Doris. "I hope I did okay, you know, fighting and . . . being the groom."

Doris doesn't look like she's going to hand out any compliments, so I step in. "You did great. Thanks again for helping out."

"Oh, sure." He bobs his head. "Let me know if you need me to do it again."

"We do have more shoots coming up so I'll let you know." I turn to Doris. "Isn't that great that Noah can help out more?"

She shrugs, stoically chewing another cookie. What is up with her? She's suddenly acting strange. Margaret looks puzzled, too.

"Okay," Noah says, "guess I better get going. Bye-bye. Bye, Doris."

"Bye." Her voice is flatter than a steamrollered pancake.

Noah shambles off, looking dejected. Okay, time to find out what's going on here. I squint up at the sun. "So, Doris, isn't it nice Noah was able to play the romantic lead with you?"

Margaret, Lizzy, and Alyssa perk up, their twelve-year-old radars beeping like crazy.

"He gets slimed," Doris says. "I don't think that's very romantic."

"What *do* you think is romantic, then?" Alyssa asks.

Doris shrugs. "I don't know. Rainbows?"

Rainbows? This girl needs to get out more.

"That's funny," Margaret says innocently. "Didn't God create the rainbow for Noah, after he survived the flood in his ark?"

"Aha," I say in a knowing voice. "For *Noah*."

Doris looks confused. "Huh?"

Lizzy throws up her hands. "Let's put it as a math equation. If rainbows are romantic, and rainbows are for Noah, then you must think Noah is romantic."

We all grin at Doris. Her cheeks are two bright spots of pink and her chin trembles a bit. "What are you talking about?"

"We're talking about, do you like Noah Fleming?" Alyssa was never one to beat around the bush.

Doris frowns, checking her folders and straightening her books. "Noah and I are friends. That's all."

"There's nothing wrong with liking him," I point out. "He's pretty cute."

"For a geek nerd," Lizzy inserts.

"He is not a geek nerd," Doris flares. "Just because he's extremely intelligent and loves science and math . . ." She trails off. "Well, he's a geek maybe, but not a nerd."

"Come on, Doris," Margaret says. "We're your friends. You can tell us."

We all waited with bated breath. We already know the answer but we need to hear it from her lips. We need Doris to admit that she thinks about something other than theorems and hypotenuses.

"Do you think he's cute?" Alyssa asks. "And don't say you've never noticed!"

"I guess so." Doris narrows her eyes. "So is Jake Knowles."

Ouch, a direct hit. Alyssa takes it without blinking. Once she gets the whiff of romance, she's like a bloodhound, nose to the trail, unstoppable. "So, you think he's cute, and we know you have stuff in common, Mobil Strips and all that..."

"Möbius Strips," Doris says in a pained voice.

"And you're always talking about math and science together. Don't deny it!" Lizzy crows.

You would think we had all spent hours practicing this frontal assault, but we've never discussed it before this minute. It's just an inborn instinct, I guess. We're working her over like some poor chump being grilled in a lawyer flick. Doris is flushed and breathless. She's probably never had a conversation like this in her life.

Margaret sighs. "Noah obviously likes you."

Nice one, Margaret. Everyone is more interested in someone who likes them back.

"Your face is red," Alyssa points out. "Like, tomato."

"It is not!" Doris practically shouts. "And I do not like Noah Fleming! He bugs me!"

Hmm, that's odd. On Saturday, she definitely liked him. Margaret opens her mouth, then shuts it. We need to regroup. I'm trying to find a tactful way to ask Doris what happened, when Paul suddenly jumps in a slush puddle right behind me. Blake laughs as the dirty water splashes against my legs.

"What is your problem?" I shout at Paul. He just shoves his hands in his pockets, grinning. His eyes slide over to Margaret.

"Hey, Margie, I've got a question for you. What do you and a pirate have in common?"

The way Blake is smiling gives me a bad feeling. Margaret turns away but Paul isn't about to be ignored. "Come on, Red," he says loudly. "You and a pirate. What's the answer?"

"Go away, Paul," I tell him. We all turn our backs on him but he just talks even louder. Other kids start to glance over.

"Why is Margaret Yorkel like a pirate? Does anyone know?"

Now he's got everybody's attention. Paul is loving it. "I'll tell you why!" he practically shouts. "It's because they both have a sunken chest!"

Some of the boys nearby snicker. A few girls do, too. My blood feels like it freezes in my veins. How can some boys be so mean? Margaret's face grows bright red and her lower lip trembles. Alyssa's and Lizzy's eyes open wide in horror and Doris is staring at Paul like he's a new breed of cockroach she just discovered. But none of us can think of a single thing to do. And these are the boys Tristan chose as friends? My blood goes from cold to hot just remembering how he used them to steer kids away from my movie.

"Shut up, Paul!" I shout, which is pretty lame and useless.

We close in on Margaret and herd her away before he can say any other stupid things. "He's such an idiot," I mutter. "Don't even pay attention, Margaret."

"How can I ignore him?" Margaret blurts. She gazes at us, close to tears. "Did you hear that? He said it in front of all those kids, and the boys were laughing!"

Margaret is right. This cannot go on. I don't know how she has stood being bullied for so long but I don't like it one bit. It's like the cold splash of muddy water has jolted me awake. I'm not spending the rest of seventh grade and all of next year being tormented, and Margaret isn't, either.

"Something needs to be done about them," I announce. "Those two have been getting away with this stuff for way too long. We need to shut them down."

"How?" Alyssa says. "They're like two-legged pit bulls."

"Exactly." I gaze solemnly at all of them. "That's why we need a plan."

"I hope you don't mean a plan to get them in trouble." Alyssa gives me a meaningful look. She's probably remembering a certain plan I concocted last semester to cause problems for her after our big fight. The plan backfired and almost ended our friendship.

"No, not in trouble." I pause, thinking about it. What *do* I mean?

"If you really want to stop them," Doris says, "you have

to threaten something they value. You know, hit them where it hurts."

Suddenly, Doris sounds more like a mob boss than a twelve-year-old science genius. I pull my coat more tightly around me. The sun has gone under a cloud and suddenly it feels cold. "I don't know anything that's important to those two, except being jerks."

"They're both on the baseball team," Lizzy says. "And remember the school assembly earlier this year? Coach said he would bench any of his players who are caught bullying."

Alyssa shrugs. "So what? If you complain to the coach, Paul and Blake will find out and they'll be twice as bad as they are now. And it's your word against theirs. The coach doesn't want to lose them so he isn't going to do anything without proof. Just forget about it."

Margaret frowns at her. Alyssa doesn't have much experience being picked on, so it's easy for her to dismiss the idea. I wish she would sound a little more concerned about Margaret. Still, Alyssa's words make sense. Even I know that tattling is the kiss of death. Telling the principal or the coach will only make things worse.

We stand in a pool of gloom. It seems like a hopeless cause. I wish there were some way to cheer up Margaret but no inspirational words come to mind, and it's time to leave. Lizzy and I wave to the others and head for the number ten bus. Neither of us feels much like talking, so I flop low in the seat, pop in some earbuds, and crank up a song on my iPod. The music can't drown out the big question swirling in my head, though. How can I put two bullies out of business and beat out a New York know-it-all?

Usually, I love teacher in-service days. There's nothing better than snoozing in bed on a day when you should be toiling in school. When I wake up Wednesday morning, though, I don't feel lazy and relaxed. The scene of Paul and his horrible joke replays in my head until I get so mad that I'm wide awake. If only I could figure out a different ending, a happily ever after where Paul and Blake get what they deserve and leave us alone. I can't help wondering if those two still make fun of my movie with Tristan. Is everyone laughing at me behind my back? I thrash around in bed at the thought. My mother says I shouldn't care what people think about me. It's sort of like saying I shouldn't care about breathing air. How do you do that? My eyes snap open.

There's no way I can get back to sleep now. Paul and Tristan have ruined my morning off.

My mind slips to Doris and Noah. What happened there? It was so much fun watching their little romance. I feel deprived, like my favorite TV reality show got canceled. Doris refuses to talk about it, and Noah follows her around like a puppy dog with his tail between his legs, trying to figure out what he did wrong. And then there's Tristan and Lydia. He probably has a crush on her. Most boys do. Maybe that's why he gave her the lead female role in his movie. Not that I care.

I stare at my ceiling and force myself not to think about any of them. I need to plan my shoot for this Saturday. I'm filming the scene where the flying saucer lands and Slug Man emerges. Usually I love thinking about how to set up cool shots, but it doesn't sound like fun right now. I give up trying to plan it and let my thoughts wander. Some people call it daydreaming, but I think of it as making mini movies. A script starts forming in my mind:

INT: KATE'S BEDROOM—MORNING

Wrinkled movie posters hang from yellow walls. A purple director's chair sits in one corner, piled high with clothing. Birds chirp outside the windows as the camera pans toward the bed, covered by a thick, lavender comforter.

The door creaks open. A man's webbed hand appears on the doorknob. Cue EERIE MUSIC.

A strange creature enters, half slug, half human. The comforter flies off the bed and KATE WALDEN emerges like a tiger from its den. She smoothes her rumpled locks of chestnut hair and glares at the monster with laser-green eyes.

An explosion erupts in the director's chair. Underwear flies in every direction as WILMA THE TRUSTY TERRIER rockets from the chair onto the bed, GROWLING at the foul creature.

Slug Man lunges forward and grabs Wilma! SLO-MO of Kate leaping away as he shoots venomous ooze in her direction. Kate backflips across

```
the room, grabs a Super Max,
Turbo-Charged, Blowtorch-Strength
Hair Dryer and turns it full blast
on the malignant gastropod. The
creature emits a high-pitched SCREAM
as his ooze dries up and he withers
to a shrunken skeleton. Kate hugs
Wilma and then raises her weapon,
victorious. . . .
```

A whimper interrupts my blockbuster daydream. Wilma is scratching at my door and her look clearly says, *I know you just saved me from a man-eating mollusk, but I need to do my business and I need to do it now.*

I groan. "Okay, Wilma. Just hold on."

I drag myself out of bed and catch sight of myself in the mirror. I've got some serious bedhead going on. I keep hoping my real-life hair will turn into the color of my movie hair, but it's still boring brown. Chestnut sounds so much cooler. My mother insists my eyes are the color of pea soup, which sounds like something Slug Man would spew. Laser-green has a ring to it.

When I go downstairs, my dad is sitting at the kitchen table, sipping coffee, his eyes at half-mast. It's a bad idea to say anything before his eyes are fully open, so I go outside with Wilma. It's my job to feed the hens in the morning, so I might as well get it over with. I used to hate feeding them. Now that they're not my leading ladies, I don't mind so much. In fact, after I refill their feeders, I stay and watch them. They practically run each other over trying to get to the food. Scrawny Henrietta is the only one that hangs back. In the movie *Chicken Run*, all the hens help each other so they can escape the evil Mrs. Tweedy. In our coop, things aren't quite so friendly. Every hen knows her place in the pecking order and Henrietta's place is way at the bottom. She runs up and down the feeding line but doesn't dare stick her head in because the others might bite it off.

"Hatched any evil plots lately?" I say out loud. They all ignore me. They're not about to give away any chicken state secrets. It feels kind of weird to talk to them, but not as weird as you might think. They remind me of a bunch of waddling, whining aunties as they squawk and scurry around. Aunties with secret ninja powers. "So, there are these two boys at school," I say. "I need to figure out a way to make them leave us alone. Any ideas?"

Henrietta blinks at me but the rest are too busy eating. I throw her a handful of grain. Agatha, a fat, prissy hen, tries to chase Henrietta off but I kick Agatha away. It's time Henrietta got first dibs at something. She gobbles up the grain, then skitters away to the far side of the coop. That's when I see it—a red gleam in the dark corner behind her. My heart does a backflip when I realize what it is—a glowing, red eye blinking at me! I jump up and squelch a scream, ready to race toward the house shouting, *I told you so! I told you so!* I've been right all along! We really do have a haunted henhouse!

I freeze in my tracks as the eye pulsates. The thing is, I don't remember having a one-eyed hen. I squint and slowly walk forward, my heart still thudding. It isn't a blinking demon eye at all. It's a camera. Derek the Spy Man has struck again.

It's a tiny mobile camera that can be mounted onto helmets and bicycle handlebars. Derek must have sneaked into the coop before me and hidden it in the straw. And that means he's got video of me talking to the hens! I should show my dad and bust Derek. He deserves it. Still, that's a big step. My dad would probably take away all his spy toys. I know Derek is just trying to have fun, and annoying me is the fun he loves best. I need to delete that video, though. Derek might threaten to show it to people. He might even try to blackmail me into doing his chores. Come to think of it, maybe I should just go to Dad after all.

Henrietta has inched nearer, probably hoping for another treat. How does a scrawny hen manage to look so sad? Maybe it's the missing feathers on her back where the other hens have pecked her. It's too bad we don't have a way to force them to be nicer to her. . . .

That's when it hits me with the stunning speed of a spewing slime ball. If a picture is worth a thousand words, then a video must be worth a million! I need to force Paul and Blake to be nicer to us. That means we need evidence.

Coach Morton couldn't ignore a video that shows them acting mean. To get that kind of top-secret video, we need twenty-first-century spy gadgetry. We need advanced recon tools. We need The Spy Man.

I grab Derek's camera, run inside, and hook it up to my computer. I quickly find the file, delete it, and return the camera to the chicken coop. Derek will probably scratch his head, wondering what happened. The problem is, I know he isn't about to let me borrow his expensive toys. What would convince him? It suddenly hits me. Derek will lend me his spy gear for the same reason that Paul and Blake aren't going to tease us anymore. My idea is simple, yet brilliant.

I throw another huge handful of feed on the floor. "Thanks, Henrietta!" It feels good to fend off the other hens so she can eat all the grain she wants. I hope she enjoys every moment. Because of her, I feel lighter, like I might sprout wings and fly up to the top of the barn. Life is better when you have a plan, especially one to take down two twelve-year-old troublemakers. Now all I need is an accomplice.

I'm tempted to text all my friends but I decide to tell them my idea in person. I wait until the next day at lunch. As usual, the cafeteria is noisy. Lunch Lady patrols the aisles, just waiting for someone to throw a morsel of food or leave behind a scrap of paper. The funny thing is, she never seems to catch Paul and Blake grabbing other students' food or taking financial "donations" from sixth graders. That's because they tag-team. One keeps watch while the other bullies. Well, it's time to change up the game.

"So, it will be simple," I sum up. "We use my brother's spy toys to secretly record Paul and Blake in action. Then, we show them the video and give them a warning. If they bother us anymore, we'll show it to the coach and principal. With proof like that, they would get benched for sure. Since they won't want to give up baseball, they'll have to leave us alone!"

I try to look modest as I wait for their admiration to wash over me. Instead, all my friends stare at me like I'm crazy. Some days it's tough being a visionary.

"Isn't that illegal?" Doris asks. "I don't think you're allowed to record someone unless you've asked their permission."

I try not to roll my eyes. "We're not taking them to court. The point is to show the principal what these guys are doing."

Lizzy dunks a rubbery chicken nugget in a pool of BBQ sauce. "Sounds tricky. What if they catch us? Paul would probably set our hair on fire or stuff us all into lockers."

Lizzy and Alyssa have the least reason to do anything risky. Paul and Blake pretty much leave them alone.

"It could backfire," I agree. "Anyone who doesn't want to help doesn't have to. No hard feelings."

Margaret is pursing her lips and I'm afraid she won't like the idea. She has very strong ideas about fair play. Finally, she nods. "Let's do it. This way, we're not telling on them. We're giving them a chance to reform. It will be up to them if they get in trouble or not."

I gaze around the table. "Who else?"

Lizzy nods. "I'm there."

Doris pushes up her glasses. "Count me in."

That leaves Alyssa. She's not the type to make herself a target. Alyssa blends in by flying low on the radar and not getting in anyone's way. She sighs and casts a glance at Blake and Paul two tables over. They're staring at something on Blake's phone and giggling like second graders. She rolls her eyes. "Yeah, I'm in." She doesn't sound very excited, but at least she's not backing out.

"What's the first step?" Margaret asks.

I feel like a legit spy as I lean forward. "First, we obtain our recon tools. I'll talk to my supplier. It's going to cost, though."

They all ponder this. Margaret digs into her pocket and throws a few crumpled singles on the table. Lizzy dives into her purse and pulls out a five, and Alyssa hands over three dollars. Doris grabs her backpack, extracts a coin purse, and counts out two dollars in quarters.

"Doris," I groan. "What's with all the change?"

She blinks. "Vending machines."

I tuck the money into my backpack. "I have a plan to get the spy gear but I need help." I turn to Alyssa. "What do you think, want to help me convince Derek?"

She brightens. “You mean tag-team him?”
“Yeah, like good cop, bad cop.”
Alyssa grins. “Or maybe bad cop, worse cop.”
I return her smile. “Roger that.”

13

As soon as we get to my house, Alyssa and I head for my room and I fill her in on my plan. Just in time, because we hear the wheezing, screeching brakes of Derek's school bus outside. I run into Derek's room and grab the items I need, then we head downstairs and position ourselves in the TV room, leaving the door ajar. Alyssa and I grin at each other. It feels like old times. We're experts at tag-teaming Derek. Once, when we were younger, we arrested Derek during a game of cops and robbers and tied him to a tree. We went inside for a snack, started watching TV, and forgot all about him. Then it started raining and Derek started shrieking. We tore outside but we couldn't undo the wet knots. We ran around the tree, laughing like crazy, begging Derek to stop screaming as we clawed at the rope. My dad finally had to cut him loose and I got in big trouble. Still, those were good times.

"Cops and robbers," I whisper to Alyssa.

She grins and nods. We hear Derek enter the kitchen, then the slam of the refrigerator door. That means he's headed our way. I count to three, then nod to Alyssa.

"I have something to tell you," she says loudly, "but you have to promise not to tell anyone else! It's super personal. I'd hate for it to get on Facebook or YouTube or anything."

A floorboard creaks outside the door. Just like I thought, Derek can't resist listening. I wink at Alyssa.

"You know I won't tell anyone. What is it?"

"Not here," she says. "Let's go up to your room."

"Sure. Let's make some nachos first, though. We can take them upstairs."

"Sounds good. I'm starving!"

We wait a moment, then open the door. Sure enough, Derek is gone. Alyssa and I smirk at each other. If I know my little brother, and I do know him way too well, he will jump at the chance to find out Alyssa's secret. We take our time in the kitchen and then slowly climb the stairs and head into my room.

"Okay, tell me what's going on," I call, shutting my door with a bang. I wander around the room, eating nachos and looking for the camera. I find it hidden behind a fuzzy, pink-framed photo of Wilma on my desk. I nod to Alyssa to show her where it is.

She throws herself on the bed. "Guess what Nathaniel Morgan told me last night?"

"What?"

"He told me he's totally in love with me, and then he kissed me!"

I have to turn away from the camera and bite back my smile. "Really? Is he a good kisser?"

"No, it was totally yuck! Sort of like if I had to kiss your awful little brother."

Now I'm choking back laughter. As we leave my bedroom, I say in a loud voice, "I can't believe he did that!"

We run downstairs and hide. Sure enough, Derek's door cracks open. He slips out and tiptoes into my room, then runs back into his own. I count a minute, then we creep back up the stairs, fling open his door, and march in. There he is, watching the camera video on his computer. "Thought you could spy on us, huh?" I say. "You are in big trouble."

Derek spins around, white-faced. "I wasn't spying!"

"The proof's right there." Alyssa points to the screen. "You planted your camera in Kate's room to spy on us."

"Yeah, and I found out you have a new boyfriend!" Derek puckers his lips at her. "Kissy kissy. I'm putting this on YouTube!"

I shake my head. "Remember what Dad said? No spying on me, or he's taking all that stuff away. I think you can kiss your spy toys good-bye."

Derek starts to look nervous. "I was just playing around. Don't worry, I'll delete the file." He grabs the camera and presses a button. "See?" He smiles triumphantly. "You can't prove I did anything."

Alyssa throws up her arms. "He outsmarted us!"

Derek leans back in his chair, grinning. "A good spy knows how to cover his tracks."

I stare at Derek, savoring the moment. Then I hold up my arm to show him the spy watch attached to my wrist. "This whole conversation has been recorded," I inform him.

Derek's eyes go round. "That's mine! You stole it!"

"Borrowed," I correct. "I think Dad will view that as a minor technicality after he sees how you spied on us, threatened to put it on YouTube, and then tried to destroy the evidence. I guess you're just not mature enough for spy toys."

Derek's shoulders sag. "I was just having fun. I wasn't going to do anything with the file!"

"We don't want to get you in trouble," Alyssa says sweetly. "We just need a favor."

He glares at us. "Like what?"

I lean forward. "We need to borrow all your spy gear. The camera, the watch, the sunglasses, and your tablet. Let's see, tomorrow's already Friday. We'll start on Monday. A week ought to do it."

Derek's mouth drops open, horrified. "No way!"

"You can lend them for a week, or lose them for a month. Maybe longer. Depends on what kind of mood Dad's in."

Derek sinks onto his bed. I can tell his brain is cranking, trying to find an out. "You have to pay me," he finally says. "You can't use them that long for free." He gets a crafty look on his face. "Ten dollars per item."

"Ha-ha, that is funny, Derek. Two dollars each, tops."

"That's nothing! Seven each, minimum!" He sits upright. "Why do you need them, anyway?"

"None of your business," I say smoothly. "We just do. Five each. You walk away with twenty dollars. That's my best offer. Otherwise, I set up a meeting with Dad."

"It's a sweet deal," Alyssa says. "Better take it."

Derek gives me a calculating look. "I need to know a few details before I send my equipment on a classified mission into enemy territory."

"Uh, okay."

Derek scrounges for paper, then grabs his Black Light Decoder Spy Pen. I roll my eyes at Alyssa. He takes this spy stuff way too seriously. Derek clicks the pen several times, frowning at his paper. "Okay," he says in a business-like voice, "what is the theater of operation?"

Alyssa and I exchange a blank look. Derek loudly sighs. "Where are you going to be using this stuff?"

I don't want to give Derek any information he could later use against me. On the other hand, we do need his help, and it is his gear. I fold my arms. "School."

Derek opens his eyes wide in surprise. He clicks his pen again. "That sounds dicey."

"We've scoped it out. It's a minimal security risk."

Derek writes on his pad. "Stationary or mobile targets?"

"Uh, mobile, I guess."

"You guess?" Derek barks. "You don't know?"

"Mobile targets," I say, then blurt, "What does it matter, Derek?"

"Everything matters when you're a spook." Click click. "That means spy, in case you're wondering."

"Yes, we know," I say impatiently. "We watch movies, too."

"And my code name is Spymaster," he goes on, ignoring me. "Please remember it."

Alyssa makes a noise halfway between a snort and a giggle. Derek swings around and glares at her. "Something funny, Jensen?"

Alyssa covers with a loud bout of coughing. She points at her throat. Derek writes again on his pad. "Okay, any nighttime requirements?"

Hmm. Night-vision goggles would be kind of cool. Too complicated, though. "No. Strictly a daytime operation."

"Uh-huh. Very well." Click click. "Target I.D.?" he casually asks.

"Top secret. Nice try."

"Aw, come on." Derek the super sleuth changes to Derek the annoying little brother in a spy-watch nanosecond. "I promise I won't tell," he whines. "Just tell me who you're spying on."

"No can do, Spymaster. That's a strictly need-to-know basis."

"Fine." Derek writes something more on the pad and then holds out the pen to me. "Sign here please. This is your guarantee that if my equipment is damaged, lost, or stolen, you will replace it new. And remember, if your cover gets blown, you took this stuff without my knowledge. This conversation never happened."

I sign the sheet, then count out twenty dollars and hand it to him. I had to use the last seven dollars of my movie fund, but it will all be worth it. If my plan works, Blake and Paul will soon be the stars of their very own crime drama.

14

Before we can outwit Paul and Blake, I have an important shoot to get ready for. When I Google flying saucers, I find lots of photos of UFOs. It's kind of creepy. According to the Internet, we must get visited by aliens every other week. The earliest is a black-and-white photo from 1870. It's supposed to be a UFO snapped near a mountaintop in New Hampshire. The summit looks more like a mound of whipped cream, though, and the UFO looks like a partly smoked cigar.

I also find a black-and-white movie from the 1950s called *Plan 9 from Outer Space*. It was made by Ed Wood, and it's so bad that it's been called The Worst Movie Ever Made. Ever. I feel kind of sorry for this Ed Wood guy, until I see all the

Web sites about him. His movies were so terrible that he's now more famous than ninety-nine percent of Hollywood directors. I guess he didn't do too badly after all.

Anyway, in *Plan 9 from Outer Space*, alien spacecraft visit Earth and turn dead humans into zombies. Ed Wood's budget was probably even smaller than mine, because he used toys for his flying saucers, and dangled them in front of the camera with fishing line. I'm pretty sure I can do a little better than Ed. Instead of using a toy, I have my dad punch a small hole in the bottom of a plastic bowl. We thread it with fishing line, leaving a big knot inside the bowl so the line won't pull through. Next, I glue the bowl upside down on a plate and paint the whole thing silver. It looks pretty cool, and when I swing it around, the fishing line hardly shows.

Something's still missing, though. I dig through our Christmas decorations, find a battery-operated strand of blinking lights, and string it on. It's perfect. My glowing, flashing flying saucer is ready to invade Earth.

As soon as I mention flying saucers, all my friends want to help with the shoot. None of the boys can make it, so Alyssa agrees to be Slug Man, since she's the tallest. After she goes into the bathroom to get into the costume, I explain to Margaret, Doris, and Lizzy how we're going to shoot the scene. As I talk, I can't help thinking about Tristan. He's shooting the first scenes of his movie today. That means Lydia, Jake, and all the others will spend the day together having fun. A stab of jealousy shoots through me. Will they talk about my movie? Will Tristan make fun of it in front of Lydia and her pals? Alyssa the Slug Man jumps into the room just then, growling like a dog. We'll need to work on that.

Margaret and Doris help me set up my dad's ladder. I tie the saucer's fishing line onto the end of a broomstick and hand it to Lizzy, my special effects coordinator. She climbs up the ladder and holds out the broomstick so the saucer dangles below. Doris and Margaret hang on to the ladder to make sure it doesn't topple over. I set up my camera on a beanbag on the ground, pointed upward. In my viewfinder, it looks like the saucer is flying against blue sky. Lizzy slowly moves it back and forth while I shoot.

"That's so cool!" Alyssa shouts, watching over my shoulder. "It's a UFO!"

"Okay, just hold it still now," I direct Lizzy. "Like it's hovering. Wait, pull it up more. The broom's in the shot!"

"My arms are about to fall off," Lizzy groans, yanking the broomstick higher. "This thing gets heavy after a while."

"I'll take a turn," Margaret offers.

"I would," Doris says, "but I have a fear of heights."

This girl has no problem plunging her fingers into frog guts in Biology, but she's afraid to climb up a ladder? I glance at her. "Really?"

"It's called acrophobia," Doris informs us. "Acrophobia is an irrational fear of heights."

"Is there such a thing as an irrational fear of frog guts?" I ask. "I think I have that."

"Ranidaphobia," Doris promptly answers. We all stare at her. Sometimes Doris is a little scary. "It's a fear of frogs. I did an extra-credit report on amphibians once. Here's a weird fact. A lot of times, people get that phobia after seeing frogs die violently. One woman developed it after she ran over a couple frogs with her lawn mower."

Alyssa makes a noise like she's going to gag.

"Yuck!" I shout. "That's horrible!"

"I am going to barf on your head," Lizzy warns Doris from above.

Only Margaret looks strangely unfazed. "My dad ran over a frog once," she admits. "It was sad."

Doris exhales huffily. "You asked me, so I told you."

Just the thought of poor, tender, innocent frogs getting creamed by a lawn mower makes my stomach twist. If I didn't have ranida-whatever before, I do now. "Let's just keep moving," I say weakly. "It's time for Slug Man to emerge from the saucer."

Alyssa raises her eyebrows. "You realize that's impossible, right?"

"We will achieve this shot by using a technique called *forced perspective*," I say in my important Hollywood director's voice. "Steven Spielberg used this trick in *Close Encounters of the Third Kind*." I pause to let the magnitude of this sink in. "Please observe carefully."

I hold up three of my mother's fat votive candles, which I've painted silver. When I first built my saucer, I attached three small pieces of Velcro to the bottom. I did the same to the candles. Now, I attach the candles to the saucer. My spacecraft's landing gear is in place.

"Margaret, Lizzy, and Doris, I need you to take this ladder and put it against that tree." I point to a tree in the middle of our yard, about forty yards off. "Prop it at a sharp angle so Alyssa can walk down facing front, like she's walking down steps."

They haul off the ladder, giving me dubious looks.

"You want me to walk down a ladder facing front in a slug suit?" Alyssa yelps. "I'll fall and kill myself!"

This is why Alyssa is such a good actress. She has a flair for the dramatic.

"I only need you to walk down the last three steps," I explain. "It's at an angle, so it shouldn't be too hard. And if you fall, at least you're close to the ground." I pick up two walkie-talkies that I rented from Derek and hand one to Alyssa. I press the button on one and the second walkie-talkie crackles.

"Cool." Alyssa puts on the slug mask, grabs the second walkie-talkie, and follows the others.

They finally reach the tree and prop up the ladder. Because it's so far away, it looks tiny in my viewfinder. I hang the saucer from a low tree branch and frame my shot so it appears huge, filling the entire left side of the frame. I adjust the camera until the far-off ladder is hidden by one of the saucer's stumpy landing legs. Feeling like a real Hollywood director, I press the walkie-talkie button. "Okay, Alyssa, get on the fourth rung. When I cue you, slowly walk down. Let's see how it looks."

"Roger that," Alyssa answers in her best, professional walkie-talkie voice.

A moment later, the two-way blares again. "Roger Dodger!" Lizzy yells. I can hear her laughing, even without the walkie-talkie.

"Roger Rabbit!" This time it's Margaret. I see her toss the two-way to Doris. Maybe I should have mentioned something about not throwing the equipment.

"Mr. Rogers' Neighborhood." Doris's flat voice crackles through the air. I can hear the others giggling behind her.

Alyssa has grabbed the two-way again. "Roger Reardon!"

Roger Reardon is a lumpy eighth grader whose face has started sprouting hairs. He calls it a beard but we call it yuck.

"Roger shut up," I radio back. The walkie-talkie sputters. I have to admit, it's kind of fun to use.

Alyssa shouts something else but the cheap electronic speaker distorts her voice and I can't understand a word. She sounds like an evil alien screaming gibberish. The chickens screech in the coop and run around in circles, flapping their wings. The noise makes them nervous. If they were cows, they would probably stampede.

Suddenly, it's like my mind does a quick rewind. *An*

Evil Alien Screaming Gibberish. That's exactly what I need! I was going to keep Slug Man silent because not even my dad could come up with a scary enough sounding voice. Alyssa screaming through the walkie-talkie sounds terrifying. Maybe Slug Man can talk after all! The best part is, I can record Alyssa and then add in the noise whenever I want. Slug Man doesn't have much of a mouth, so I don't have to worry about matching moving lips. I squint toward the far tree, where they're all laughing as they fight for the two-way. My professional film crew has turned into a bunch of six-year-olds squabbling over a toy.

"Alyssa, get up on the ladder!" I bark into the walkie-talkie.

I think maybe Alyssa sticks out her tongue at me, but I'm too far away to tell. It doesn't matter, because she climbs up and gets in position. I feel a tiny thrill run through me as I peer at my viewfinder. Will this trick work? Right now, Alyssa and the ladder are both hidden by the spaceship.

"Okay, action!" I radio.

Like magic, a small Alyssa appears from the side of the huge saucer and slowly descends to the ground.

I grab the walkie-talkie. "It looks AMAZING!" I shout. Suddenly, they're all running toward me. Even Alyssa lumbers along in the slug suit. "Wait!" I radio. "We need to do it again!"

It's too late. They all want to see it. They crowd around the viewfinder as I replay the shot.

“Wow,” Alyssa says. “Look at me! It’s perfect!”

“You’re so cute!” Lizzy cries to Alyssa. “Like a cute little alien, climbing down from your ship to kill us all!”

“That’s an awesome shot, Kate,” Margaret tells me.

I grin happily, trying to look modest. It *is* a pretty genius idea. Of course, it isn’t mine. It’s old-school Hollywood at its best. We’re all laughing and joking as we watch it again. Suddenly, my cell phone beeps. I’ve got a text from a number I don’t recognize. *Hope yr shoot going good as mine. We’re shooting shooting :)*

Tristan. I can’t believe he’s texting me. My friends must see the look on my face, because they crowd around to read the text. Everyone quiets down. I can feel them furtively glancing at me while pretending to check their own phones. They all know about the sign-up sheet fiasco. And I’ve let drop a few comments about Tristan’s know-it-all attitude. Okay, maybe it was more than a few comments. Maybe I ranted for an entire lunch period once. Nobody mentions Tristan in my presence anymore.

“Shooting shooting?” I mutter. “What does that even mean?”

Tristan also sent a photo. It’s Jack Timner, Jake, and some other guys dressed in suits and sunglasses, fedoras pulled low over their eyes, posing with guns. They must be filming a shoot-’em-up scene. They look cool. Alyssa gazes over my shoulder and I think I hear her sigh. That makes me feel even worse. My phone beeps again and a second photo pops up. It's a selfie of Tristan with Lydia. She's all glammed up in a vintage dress and hat, with lots of makeup, her arm slung loosely around Tristan's shoulders, laughing.

I want to act like it's no big deal because, really, it *is* no big deal. It's just a stupid text and a couple photos. So why does it make me so mad? I can't even get away from Tristan on weekends now. Compared to what he's doing, my big special effects shot suddenly seems stupid. It's just someone in a silly costume pretending to creep out of a big plate with an upside-down bowl on top of it.

"We should send Tristan a photo!" Margaret pipes up.

"Yeah," Lizzy chimes in. "All of us, with Alyssa in the suit!"

I stick my phone in my pocket. "Are you kidding? He's just gloating." The last thing I want Tristan to see is my slug man costume. I'd probably hear him and his new friends laughing all the way from his big house in Deer Hollow.

Doris shrugs, "Maybe he's not gloating. Maybe he's just..." She vaguely waves a hand in the air. "Maybe he's just saying hello."

"Hope your shoot's going good as mine," I mimic. "What does that sound like? He's showing off. Look at me, this is how great my shoot is! He's just trying to make me feel bad."

"But our shoot is going great, too," Alyssa points out. "Isn't it?"

I bat at the flying saucer with my hand and it swings crazily on the fishing wire. I must have hit it too hard because two of the landing legs fall off. "Yeah, sure." I try to give them a big smile but it feels like someone popped all the balloons in the middle of a party, dragged in a body, and started a funeral service.

I can't help remembering how Lydia and her friends all bragged about me the day I met Tristan. They hung on my every word. I had carved out my place at Medford Junior High. Everybody knew I was the girl who was crazy about making movies. I was the future film director. Lydia even called me *Hollywood*. Well, it's a known fact that Hollywood knows way more about movies than New York. The weather is way better, too. So that's it, then. It's simple. I need to figure out a way to keep this know-it-all New Yorker from raining all over my parade... *and* my movie. To do that, I just need to win one little award. How hard can it be?

Monday dawns cold and foggy—kind of like my mood after seeing those photos of Tristan's movie shoot. At least it's perfect spy weather. Blake and Paul won't know what hit them. The thought cheers me as I pull a few slick James Bond moves in front of the mirror. The theme song from some old 007 movie plays in my head. I kind of wish my friends and I all had code names, but that would be too corny to suggest. I've called a special before-school meeting so we can plant our new spy tools without anyone noticing. We only have a week, so every moment counts.

"What project are you working on so early in the morning?" my dad asks in the car. He's driving me to school before going to work. He's in his usual shirt and tie, looking bleary-eyed. Monday morning mud mind, he calls it.

He grips a cup of coffee in one hand and the steering wheel with the other.

"Uh, it's about the correct installation and procedures for digital recording devices and how that can be beneficial to population security. You know, extracurricular stuff."

My dad nods his head. "Uh-huh. Okay." He sips his coffee and squints out the window.

I smile to myself. I told the truth and he didn't even blink. Just call me the Disinformation Specialist. The CIA will be knocking on my door any day now, begging me to join their ranks. If I didn't want to be a Hollywood director so badly, I would consider a career in espionage. Then I could wear glamorous jewels and take down shady underworld characters with a swift kick of my stiletto heels. Actually, it sounds like just the kind of movie I'd love to make someday.

I wear Derek's sunglasses to our early morning meeting. Lizzy raises her eyebrows. "Where'd you get those shades?"

"They were my grandmother's," I say blandly. "Cool, huh?"

"Uh, yup."

"They're kind of retro," Margaret says politely.

I can tell they think I've made a poor fashion choice. Doris just yawns. I've decided to install the tiny spy camera in Margaret's locker since she gets picked on the most. We hide it inside a plastic figurine of a pig that she keeps on her top shelf. Margaret adores pigs, which seems like a strange animal for a neat freak to love, but she insists pigs are clean and only roll in mud to stay cool. She also says they're more intelligent than dogs. I'm pretty sure Wilma is way smarter than any pig, though. The pig is yawning, kind of like Doris. We tape the camera inside its mouth. All Margaret has to do is reach behind the pig and turn it on.

Since Doris spends the most time with Margaret during the day, I hand her Derek's Spytech wristwatch and show her how to use it. We only have ten more minutes before the bell rings. I need to wrap this up. "And now for our third spy tool." I pull off the sunglasses with a flourish and plug them into Derek's tablet. That gets everybody's attention. They squeal when they see our entire recorded conversation.

"That's amazing!" Margaret says. "Spy shades!"

"Pretty cool," Lizzy admits.

I unplug the sunglasses. "I'll be using these. They should come in handy if Paul and Blake bother us outside." I tuck the sunglasses away. "Okay ladies, this is it." My friends are clustered around me in a loose huddle. I wish an inspirational speech would pop into my head like in the sports movies where the coach says the perfect thing and the team surges from behind and wins the game. Nothing comes to mind. "We've got a week to do this," I finally say. "So let's get out there and catch us some bad boys."

We all split up and I head for my locker. As I'm pulling out books, I spot Lydia cruising down the hall, four girls revolving around her like planets. She's going on and on about how much fun Tristan's shoot was on Saturday, and what a great director he is, and how his parents bought everyone gourmet take-out pizza from Don Bernatello's and ice cream from Twisters.

"Lydia is the star of the whole thing," Tina Turlick chimes in, as if the other girls didn't already know that.

"Well, really Jack is," Lydia says. "He's the detective. I'm his lady love, except I'm secretly trying to kill him."

I'm hiding inside my locker, pretending to search for something buried deep, deep within its depths. If I push hard enough against all the winter coats and sweaters, maybe I'll just keep going, like Lucy in *The Lion, the Witch and the Wardrobe*. I press against the back, just in case there's a forest lurking back there. I don't feel any snowflakes, though, just cold hard metal, which means I can't escape Lydia's blaring voice.

"You should have seen the gun battle scene! Tristan bought some fake blood and he put some in a little balloon and gave it to Carter Walters to pop under his shirt when he gets killed. All this blood comes gushing out like his guts got ripped open! Tristan's a genius. I told him he's going to be the next Peter Jackson, minus the beard. I told him, please, dude, no beard."

She whips out her cell phone to show them a photo of the bloody Carter Walters. I hear *oohs* and *ahhs* from her fan club.

"Big deal!" I sneer. "I've made blood by the buckets.

Only an amateur buys it at the store!" I don't say this to them, of course. I mutter it under my breath while I'm digging in my locker, hoping not to be noticed. I know what Lydia is really saying. What she really means is that Tristan is a way better director than me. She never said what a great director I am. If I were to pop out now, there would be a big awkward silence, some grins, maybe even stifled tittering. Lydia played a zombie for my first movie but I had to cut the scene. I chased her and Alyssa around in a cornfield for what seemed like hours, trying to get a decent shot. Was it my fault they wouldn't listen? Now, Tristan flashes his smile and buys gourmet pizza and everybody's dying to do whatever he tells them.

I can only stay crouched down for so long. I've already uncovered late math homework, an earring missing since September, and a crumpled but unused piece of bubble gum, which I pop in my mouth. Finally, Lydia and her gang move on. I'm about to stand up when a shadow falls over me. A tiny worm of dread burrows into my stomach. I fumble for the sunglasses in my pocket but when I turn around, it's just Margaret.

The first bell goes off but she doesn't move. She has a strange kind of wistful look on her face. "Paul just called me Buttface." She says this matter-of-factly. "And Stork Legs."

"That's perfect!" It feels weird to be excited that Paul is calling her names. "I mean, you know, it's just the kind of thing we need."

"I was four feet from my locker," Margaret goes on. "By the time I did the combination, opened it up, and turned on the camera, he was already gone." She hesitates. "I don't know, Kate. It's going to be really hard to catch them in the act."

"Are you kidding?" I exclaim. "It's only the first day. We have three spy cameras. They'll mess up and we'll be there. Don't worry. By the end of the week, we'll have enough footage on those guys to make an entire movie."

Margaret smiles but she doesn't look convinced, which just shows how smart she is.

As it turns out, catching bullies is way trickier than it looks. It's almost like Paul and Blake know we're trying to snare them. They tease Margaret everywhere *except* at her locker. They mount rapid-fire attacks and move on before Doris can turn on her spy watch. I practically throw myself into their path, but it's like I'm invisible. Paul and Blake walk right past, hurrying to get to baseball practice or catch a bus.

Friday rolls around and we have no video. Zero. Nada. By the end of the day, I'm pretty depressed. How do those reality TV shows always get such great footage? My plan was an epic fail. As I'm heading for my bus, I spot Paul and Blake hanging on the outer edge of a bunch of kids. I think about slipping on my sunglasses and trying to get their attention, but the group also includes Tristan and Lydia. No way am I making myself a target. Still, I slow down as I draw near. For some reason, I just have to know what they're all talking about.

"I can't believe Jack got in trouble again," I overhear Tristan say to Lydia. "They nailed him for pulling the fire alarm."

So that's why we had a fire drill this morning. If I know Jack, he probably had a group of boys egging him on.

"No way!" Lydia screeches. "That was Jack? I'll have to thank him for getting me out of History!"

"The principal called his parents and they grounded him," Tristan goes on. "So he can't shoot with us this weekend. It's too bad, there's one shot I really need to redo. Jack ended up way too dark. I've gotta figure out how to get more light in that room."

I catch my breath. I know about light. This is my big chance! It's time to show up Tristan for the fake he is. The thought of approaching this big group of kids is nerve-racking, but it's now or never. I steel myself, put on a nonchalant face, and amble over. "Did I hear you're having a lighting problem?"

Tristan gives me a big, two-faced smile. "Just a shot that's too dark."

"You know, I've had lighting problems before, too. Why don't you try an Elvis," I suggest. "Or maybe a Lisa Marie."

Everybody's gaze ping-pongs from me to Tristan. The look on his face is worth all the mind-numbing hours I've spent memorizing film lingo. He doesn't have any idea what

I'm talking about. He kicks at an invisible pebble, buying time. Finally, he pushes back his hair and squints at me. "Uh, sounds familiar." He scratches his nose. "So, remind me, what are those again?"

I was going to play this casual, maybe just let my eyes go a little wide, but I get carried away in the moment. "You don't know what an Elvis is?" My voice is a little sharper than I intend. A little meaner. Tristan's face flushes. Still, everyone is quiet, listening to me, Kate Walden, teach the New York snob a little something he doesn't know about the film business.

"An Elvis is a reflector made with gold fabric," I say loudly. Even the bus drivers can probably hear me. "It's named after Elvis Presley because that's how he used to dress. Really flashy. A Priscilla is a silver reflector, named after his wife, and a Lisa Marie has silver and gold blocks together. Because, you know, Lisa Marie is their kid."

I bask in the awed silence that follows my explanation. It feels great, like I just took a giant chomp out of the Big Apple.

Then Paul opens his mouth. "Yeah, right. I bet you just made that up."

"No, I didn't," I reply, stung. "It's what all the film crews call them."

"Hand me an Elvis Presley," Paul says in a moronic clown voice.

"Where's my Lisa Marie?" Blake squeaks in falsetto. "Pass me a pretty Priscilla!"

Paul curls his lips at me. "That's the stupidest thing I've ever heard."

Now, everyone is grinning, and Paul will probably blurt out my nickname any second. Tristan is about to chime in but I cut him off.

"Actually, Paul, *you're* the stupidest thing you've ever heard," I retort, not even caring if it makes sense. I stalk off toward the bus before Paul can reply. I hear muffled titters from the girls. Why does being a know-it-all work so well for Tristan and not for me?

The sun slips behind a cloud with perfect Hollywood timing. If this were a movie scene, the colorist would tint it blue, as in depressed. As I sink into a bus seat, I overhear two guys behind me talking about Tristan's movie, and how Jack did such a great job, and Tristan is so nice, blah blah blah. I've overheard it in the girls' bathroom, in the hallway, in the cafeteria. Awesome. Fun. Great. Dude. It's like no one has anything else to talk about. Don't these kids have hobbies?

As Sal pops the clutch into gear and pulls out of the parking lot, a sunless chill creeps inside me. I just looked like an idiot in front of Tristan, again. Even worse, my friends and I are out twenty bucks and we don't have a single, solitary *Crapkate* or *Margerine* to show the principal.

An entire week rolled past and I didn't nail any of my targets. Maybe I'm not cut out for espionage after all. Derek's been complaining to me all week about not having his toys, so I know he won't give me more time, and I don't have any money left to buy my own spy gear.

As soon as I get home, I put Derek's stuff on his bed and walk out to the chicken coop. I lean against the wall of the outdoor pen, watching the hens scratch in the dirt. I was so sure Henrietta's plan would work. Derek's bus pulls up, wheezing like it has a bad case of asthma. I watch as he swings off and heads into the house. For some reason, I feel like just sitting and watching the hens. I throw them some grain and they run over and peck at it. Their lives are so uncomplicated. Hungry. Eat. Tired. Sleep. I wish my life could be that simple. Paul and Blake will always be lurking now, just waiting to humiliate me and make fun of my movies. Except I won't be making another movie because, with Tristan around, I'll be too embarrassed. What if nobody wants to be in it?

The kitchen door opens and Derek trudges toward me, wearing his sunglasses and spy watch. He stares at the chickens, then at me. "What's the matter? You look like a hen just laid an egg on your face."

Normally I would say something witty like, *At least I have a face*, or *At least my face doesn't look like somebody scrambled it*. Somehow, I don't have the energy. I throw the hens some more grain. "Ha-ha, that's funny."

He taps his watch. "Did you get what you needed?"

I take a deep breath. "Funny thing. We came close a couple times but we couldn't nail them. I was just wondering . . ."

"Nope," Derek says right away. "No more time. You had all my stuff for a week. That's like forever!"

"Fine, whatever." I throw some more grain to the hens.

"You wanna play Mario?"

"No. Just leave me alone, okay?"

Derek stands there, watching me. "You know, a lot of people think being a spy is easy, but it's not. So don't feel bad. Even James Bond has a tough week sometimes." He heads back toward the house.

"James Bond has it easy," I mutter. "He's not a seventh-grade girl."

Henrietta bobs her head and clucks like she agrees with me. It occurs to me that she's probably a middle schooler too, in chicken years. She gets bullied and, as hard as she tries, nothing ever works out for her. For some reason, this makes me so sad that a few tears leak from my eyes. Poor Henrietta.

Margaret is especially sad that we didn't manage to nail Paul and Blake. She's quieter than normal at school. I feel like her unhappiness is my fault. If I hadn't come up with the spy gear idea, she never would have gotten her hopes up. I try not to think about our failed effort. Instead, I focus on the film festival deadline, which is coming up fast. I've decided what my movie really needs is a big chase scene to impress the judges. That means it's time to move off the farm. I want a gritty, urban Batman-style setting. The best that dull downtown Medford offers is two blocks on the edge of town lined with warehouses, bars, and grimy storefronts. I choose Franklin Street, home to a tattoo parlor called Blink & Ink. It's sandwiched between the Medford

Thrift Mart on one side and a tavern called Crow Bar on the other.

This is where my cast and crew meet up on Saturday morning. After Noah arrives, he speed-walks in wide circles around Doris, casually whistling but not daring to get too close. His off-key melody starts getting on my nerves so I make him put on the slug man outfit. He still whistles, but it's muted.

"Noah, don't forget your glasses," I remind him. "You need to wear them."

He pulls them out of his pocket and wedges them on his nose.

A few cars cruise past and the passengers stare at us. Mostly, they stare at Noah in the costume. An old guy stumbles out of the Crow Bar as we're setting up. He rubs his whiskery chin and squints at Noah. "Ha-ha, is it Halloween today? Hoo, look at the claws on that thing."

We all look to my dad, who's leaning against the back of our car, sipping his coffee. He stands up and ambles over. "It's for a movie they're shooting."

"A movie?" the old man cries. "Well, you can shoot me! I always wanted to be in a movie." He throws his arms wide and does a little jig. His T-shirt looks like it used to be white a long time ago, before they invented washing machines. There's something sad and a little scary about him, even though he's just an old man. Maybe it's his grizzled chin, or the ropy muscles in his arms, or the wrinkly tattoos that look like purplish melanomas creeping across his skin. He looks like a character out of a movie.

A huge, blinding lightbulb pops inside my head. A guy like this is just what my movie needs! Lots of big sci-fi blockbusters include a down-and-out street bum who mumbles strange prophecies that turn out to be true. It adds cinematic style. The judges will love it. And this guy wants to do it. Just because he's had some hard times doesn't mean we should be afraid of him. He could be a great actor. I could be discovering the next Leonardo DiCaprio! Or, more like Leonardo's down-on-his-luck uncle.

"I always wanted to be in a movie," he repeats. "I was in a play in fifth grade, *Julius Caesar*."

"Uh, thanks, but all the parts are already taken." My dad puts his hand on Noah's shoulder. He's smiling and amiable, but I notice he gently pulls Noah back a step. Now, my dad is between Noah and the old man.

"I might have one part you could play," I announce.

My dad gives me a look. Roughly translated, it means *cease and desist*. I pretend not to notice. I've got to make this movie perfect. My brain is whirling, trying to come up with an idea. "Just a small part." I glance at my dad. "A really small part."

"You mean old Leo's going to be in a movie?" the man cries.

I catch my breath. "Is your name Leo?"

"That's right. Leo Hoffman."

I look at Alyssa to see if she has registered the magnitude of this moment. He has the same name as one of my all-time favorite actors! It must be a sign. Leo is meant to be in my movie. Alyssa is staring at me like I've just turned into a slug, complete with tiny slug brain. She's shaking her head and mouthing something at me. Okay, she obviously didn't catch the significance. I guess that's why I'm the director.

"Ha-ha, look what I can do!" Leo concentrates really hard, almost crossing his eyes, then grins at us. "Didja see that?"

We all exchange wondering glances. I can tell Lizzy is trying hard not to laugh.

"I think we missed it," Margaret says in her polite, adult voice.

"Hey, that's pretty cool," Noah says. He pulls off the slug head and grins at Leo. "My uncle can do that, too."

"What could you possibly see with your head stuck inside that mask, with those little slits for eyes?" Doris asks crossly, as if he's making it up.

Noah giggles. "Watch his ears."

Leo points to his saggy, creased earlobes. He scrunches his wrinkly forehead like he's thinking really hard, and suddenly his ears waggle up and down. "I can do that for your movie."

Noah giggles again. My dad looks like he's lost in a foreign country, wishing he had a map. He gulps the last of his coffee and smiles at Leo. "Very impressive. But I don't think that's what—"

"That is so cool!" I cry, even though waggling ears isn't what I have in mind. I want a close-up of this guy and I need to do something fast before my dad shuts me down. What would Peter Jackson do? He'd probably stick some hair on Leo's feet and call him a hobbit. Leo is still grinning and wiggling his ears at us. He's missing a few teeth, which is even more perfect. I need to give him some lines.

"Okay, this is a chase scene," I tell him. "So, Leo, Noah is going to run by in his costume. I want you to step in front of him, grab onto his arm, and say . . ." I have no idea what I want him to say. Noah looks nervous, like he doesn't want to be grabbed.

"You know," my dad says. "I don't think it's fair to expect Leo to remember lines. Why don't we just . . ."

"How about 'Beware the needle'?" I blurt. "You're warning him. So you say, 'Beware the needle.'" Another flash of inspiration hits me. "Then say, 'The snail's pace wins the race.'"

It's mysterious. It's cryptic. Not bad for off the top of my head, and it even rhymes. The judges will eat it up. I'll figure out what it means later.

"Beware the needle," Leo mumbles. "The snail's pace wins the race."

I give my dad a so-there smile. Leo's a natural. Even Alyssa usually forgets her lines the first couple times. My dad doesn't look happy so I pretend to be busy with my clipboard.

"So, Trevor and Alyssa, you're the two scientists chasing Christopher the slug creature. You want to find out where he hid Adrienne. Plus, you want to sedate him so you can try to turn him back into a human."

Trevor and Alyssa get into their lab coats as I block the scene, which means I show everyone where they're starting from and where they're running to. I stick Leo up against the stained brick wall of the Crow Bar, near a narrow alley that runs between the tavern and the next building. Noah will run up the alley, Leo will grab on to him right in front of the camera, and the others will follow. I hand Lizzy the boom mike, which is a microphone taped onto a broom handle. She holds it over Leo's head. Leo is mumbling to himself, going over his lines, no doubt. My heart is pounding with excitement. I know I'm only going to get one take, and then my dad will tell me to move on. I hope this works.

"Places, everybody!" Margaret shouts, even though everyone is already in place.

I turn on the camera and say a quick prayer. "Okay, ACTION!" I shout.

Noah races down the alleyway. He careens straight into a trash can and goes sprawling, then bounces back up and keeps running. Wow, that was pretty creative. I didn't even tell him to do that. I hear Doris snort behind me and Margaret shushes her, which sounds even louder than the snort. It's like my brain suddenly splits into three parts—one sliver is thinking that I might have to cut those sounds out later. Another part is watching through the viewfinder as Noah races toward Leo. Yet another slice of my brain is babbling something like, *Wow, I can't believe it! I'm directing a movie!*

So part of me is worrying, part is concentrating, and the other part is on an adrenaline rush, and it all happens in just a few seconds. Then, Noah reaches Leo. Just like I told him to, Leo leaps out and grabs hold of Noah's arm. He's grinning, but that's okay because it makes him look kind of crazy, with the missing teeth and grizzled cheeks.

"Beware!" he croaks. His eyes dart back and forth. Has he forgotten the line?

"Beware the Ides of March!"

Wha-at? The Ides of March? Isn't that what somebody said to Julius Caesar right before they killed him?

Leo is panting like the excitement is a little too much for him. "The snail's needle! The race is the snail!" He's clutching Noah, shaking him too hard. Noah is making noises, trying to get away, but Leo doesn't notice. He stares off, frowning, his mouth working. Then, he stomps his foot. "I forgot!" he cries. "I forgot the line!" He licks his lips, his eyes bloodshot. He's suddenly way more worked up than he should be. Or maybe he's drunker than he should be. Leo kicks a nearby trash can and swears a blue streak.

I want to tell him that it's all just for fun, it's just a kid's movie, but I can't get the words out. Everyone is staring at him, open-mouthed. My dad is already moving forward. He grabs Noah's arm and pulls him away.

"That was fine, Leo. You did great," he says soothingly. "Come on, kids, time to go."

"I can do it!" Leo says belligerently, but he's already deflating. "I should have been Brutus," he mumbles. "I wanted to be Brutus and that teacher, that Miss-What's-Her-Name made me a guard." He rubs his chin and then looks over at me. "How's that, girlie? Did you like my Brutus?"

"It was perfect." I'm packing up equipment as fast as I can. "Thanks, Leo. We'll see you later."

My dad herds us all toward the car.

"Yeah, yeah," Leo says gloomily. He turns and trudges back toward the tavern. I want to shout so many things—*Don't go in there, Leo!* Or maybe, *You would have made a great Brutus!* A part of me even wants to tell him: *Don't drink anymore, it's bad for you!* But in the end, I don't say anything. I watch Leo shove open the door and disappear inside.

After Leo vanishes into the Crow Bar, I notice Noah is on the ground, with the mask off, holding his head. Doris is crouched by him. Everyone else is staring at me. They don't look happy, especially my dad.

"That guy was so scary," Alyssa says.

Trevor gives a manly shrug. "I was wondering if I should tackle him, but I didn't want to hurt him."

"Yeah, poor guy," I say, hoping to create some sympathy for Leo and maybe for myself. "I guess he got a little too excited."

My dad cuts me off. "Bad idea, Kate." He's shaking his head. "Very bad idea." Before I can defend my director's vision, he turns to Noah. "You okay, son?"

"I'm fine." Noah's voice sounds thin, like it's been run

through a strainer. "I just feel a little nauseous." He glances at Doris. "It's probably the heat. It's really hot inside this costume."

Doris leans over him like a ministering angel. "It was probably from that guy shaking you so hard." She frowns in my direction.

Margaret puts a hand on Noah's forehead. "He's clammy," she reports. "Maybe he's going into shock."

Clearly, Margaret has watched way too many doctor shows on TV. "Shock?" I repeat. "Come on you guys, it wasn't that bad—"

Noah picks this moment to lean over and puke on the sidewalk. His ministering angel leaps away, holding her nose. She didn't need to worry about getting dirty because somehow most of the puke ends up all over my costume.

That's when I notice everyone is staring at me again like it's my fault. Which I'm pretty sure it isn't because I never told Leo to shake Noah. Maybe one third to one half, max, is my responsibility. My dad runs to get napkins from the car.

"Sorry," Noah gasps. "I have a weak stomach. That's what my mother says. I don't do well on long car rides, either. Or roller coasters. Once, on the Octopus, I—"

"Noah," Doris says. "Stop talking."

"Okay," Noah says. And he does.

My dad hands him napkins to wipe off his face. The slug suit, however, will need way more than a few napkins. My dad helps Noah out of it. He's just wearing gym shorts and a T-shirt underneath. With his long, skinny white legs, he looks like an albino stork. An embarrassed, miserable stork. I guess if I had just puked in front of my crush, I might feel bad, too.

"Sorry about that, Noah," I say. "Leo seemed so harmless. . . ."

I glance around but nobody is chiming in to back me up. Even Margaret is staring off, pretending she doesn't hear me. "Don't worry," I go on, "the next scene we're shooting will be much easier."

"That's all the shooting for today," my dad interrupts. "I think Noah has had enough."

I stare at my dad, shocked. "But we have a whole other scene to finish!"

He gives me a look and I know I'd better not argue anymore. Noah starts to hand the costume to my dad but he just points at me, so Noah dumps it at my feet.

"Sorry," he mumbles.

The costume reeks. I gingerly pick it up, trying not to look too close, because I really don't want to know what Noah had for breakfast that morning. I bet this never happens to the Wookiee shirts in the *Star Wars* movies. I take a bottle of water and pour it over the worst parts, feeling like I might just puke myself. Nobody offers to help me. When I've got it cleaned off as best I can, I roll it up and we stick it in the back of the car. My dad offers to give people lifts home, except we don't have enough room for everybody. Luckily, Lizzy says her mom is shopping downtown and can pick her up. The rest of us pile into our Suburban.

Noah sits next to Doris. He grins at the roof, not looking at her. He clears his throat, turns toward her, then coughs into his fist and resumes his painful smile at the roof. Good grief. Now that he's better, Doris has changed from ministering angel to stone gargoyle. What is up with her?

Margaret pushes up her glasses and turns to Noah. "Did you mean to fall down like that in the alley? Was that on purpose?"

I nod my head at Noah. *Just say yes*, I brain wave him. *Sound manly*.

He grins sheepishly. "It's like that trash can jumped out of nowhere! I never saw it."

"Dude, that was a stud fall," Trevor says. "You bounced up like that suit's made of rubber."

Alyssa leans forward. "Yeah, that was sweet, Noah."

Noah grins, and looks hopefully at Doris.

She frowns. "It looked like you hurt yourself." Her voice sounds accusing, like he probably hurt himself on purpose.

"Uh, I'm not sure, I don't think so. Maybe a little." Noah watches her, trying to gauge the right answer.

Doris sighs huffily. "You should be careful. You're going to rip Kate's suit."

Noah nods and stares at the car roof. I wish I could kick Doris but I'm in the front seat. I have a way to fix her, though. “Next time we shoot, it will be a scene between Christopher and Adrienne, the love of his life,” I announce.

Two spots of pink creep into Doris’s cheeks.

“Even though he’s now a slug creature,” I go on, “he’s still madly in love with her and wants to spend the rest of his life with her. He wants to have little mollusk babies with her.”

“Oooh,” Alyssa groans, trying to be funny. “That sucks.”

Noah shakes his head. “No, you know what sucks? What really, really sucks?” He giggles. “Black holes.”

Doris’s lip quivers. Noah gives her a delighted glance. He makes a loud sucking noise for us science morons. “Black holes suck everything in, get it?”

“Right,” I say. “Got it.”

Alyssa leans toward me and says under her breath, “I don’t know how many more dumb science jokes I can take.”

After we’ve dropped everyone off, I get a long lecture from my dad on the ride home about how I need to start listening better and not ignore him or I won’t be shooting any more scenes, period, and how I better not invite any more unknown, possibly drunk strangers to be in my movie, and how Noah might have gotten hurt worse. I can’t help pointing out that Noah puked, which is different than getting hurt. And how was I supposed to know Leo had been drinking, or that he was trying to relive a painful event from his childhood? My dad insists I’m arguing, even though

I'm merely pointing out facts, and he grounds me off TV for a week.

The thing is, I know my dad is about fifty percent right. I did get carried away. You could possibly even say I messed up. It's just hard to admit. I turn toward him but it's like the air between us is clogged with all the things I should have already said but can't get out. The longer I wait, the heavier the air feels, until it's hard to breathe. Finally, I slouch down in my seat and stare glumly out the window. I let down my dad, I can't watch TV, and all my friends are mad at me. Yet, as bad as I feel, one tiny sliver of my brain, the one on the adrenaline rush, is already skimming through Leo's footage in my head, hoping it looks as amazing as it did in my viewfinder.

By the time we get home from my failed shoot, the car is starting to smell. I pull the rolled up costume from the backseat, holding my nose. Derek runs out of the house and stops short. "What happened?"

"Noah got sick." I decide it's best to leave out the details.

My dad points to the water hose. "You'd better use that."

As I'm washing the costume, my mother's car pulls into the driveway. I drop the hose and run over. Our fast-food and Chinese take-out dinners were fun, but I'm really glad to see her. Even when Derek, my dad, Wilma, and I were all in the house together, it still felt empty. I give her a big hug as soon as she steps out of the car.

"What's this?" she teases. "You didn't miss me, did you?"

"Nope." I grin at her. "Not at all. How's Grandma?"

"Much better. She sends all her love."

Derek hurries over. "How was it? Did you find out about chicken intestinal diseases?"

"The conference was wonderful," she says cheerily. "I learned a lot. In fact, my head is spinning. I'm so glad to be home."

I tell her all about my shoot with Leo, leaving out the small detail that he might have had too much to drink. This reminds me that I haven't checked the mask or gloves yet to see if they were contaminated. I find the gloves in the car, but not the mask. I check all the seats and the back. I even check the glove compartment.

My dad is helping my mother carry in her suitcase. "Hey Dad, where did you put my mask?"

"I didn't put it anywhere. It should be in the car. Did you look?"

I check to see if he's fooling because my dad loves to pretend he's lost our stuff when he really hasn't. He doesn't look like he's joking, though.

"It's not there. I searched all over."

My dad frowns. "Who put it in the car?"

I shake my head, trying to remember what happened after Leo went a little crazy on us and Noah got sick. In all the confusion, I figured someone else threw the mask in the car. One of my friends must have seen it. Maybe Noah or Lizzy grabbed it and accidentally took it home with them.

I reach for my phone and start texting. Within five

minutes, I've heard back from everyone. Nobody has it. Nobody remembers seeing it or putting it into the car.

"What if you don't find it?" Derek asks. "How are you going to finish your movie? How are you going to win the prize?"

"I don't know!" I shout. I don't mean to yell at him, but the same questions are swirling inside my head and I don't have any answers. Derek looks hurt so I nudge him. "Help me look in the car again. Maybe I missed it."

We run outside and search every inch, with no luck. I race back to the house. "It's not there!" I'm still shouting. I guess it's better than crying, which is what I feel like doing.

My parents share a look. Then, my dad grabs his car keys. "Let's go. I'll bet we left it behind and it's still sitting there on the sidewalk."

My dad just spent his entire Saturday morning overseeing my shoot. He fended off an old drunk, took my friends home, and then drove half an hour to our house with a reeking costume in the backseat. My mother just got home, he barely had a chance to talk to her, and now he's ready to drive back to town to look for my mask. My dad's the best.

"I'm coming too!" Derek pipes up.

My mother gives me an apologetic smile. "I just spent five hours in the car. I think I'll stay here and unpack, but call me as soon as you find it."

We pile into the Suburban and pull out of the driveway.

My dad runs a hand through his thinning hair. I guess it's been a long day for him. When we dropped off Noah at his house, his parents were out working in the yard. My dad had to go over and tell them what happened. They didn't look pleased that an old geezer was manhandling their son. It occurs to me now that, even though I was fifty percent to blame, maybe even seventy-five percent, Noah's parents probably blame my dad. He probably blames himself. I put my dad in this awkward position and made him look like a bad parent.

"I'm really sorry, Dad," I blurt. "You know, about everything. I was being stupid. And thanks for driving me back."

My dad smiles and pats my leg. "Don't worry. The mask is probably right where we left it."

I nod. It's got to be there. Why would anyone take a slug suit mask?

Derek gazes at me with his serious, little brother eyes. "I hope you find it."

"Thanks." Sometimes he's such a sweet kid.

"That would be terrible if you didn't get to use all that slime footage. That's the best part of your movie."

"Yeah." I'm not really listening. I'm saying a prayer inside my head and it goes something like this: *please let it be there, please let it be there, please let it be there. . . .*

But it isn't. We check the sidewalk, the alleyway, all around the bench, even inside a nearby trash can. My mask has disappeared. My dad even goes into the Crow Bar while

Derek and I wait in the Suburban. When he gets back inside the car and sighs, I know it's bad news.

"They said Leo comes in every once in a while but nobody knows where he lives. And no one has seen the mask." My dad shakes his head. "I don't know. I just don't know what could have happened to it, Kate."

"It's gone," I say flatly. "It's just gone."

A big lump rises in my throat. I can't finish my movie, much less win a prize. I still have important scenes to shoot, but the star of my movie now has no face. How can I film an exciting ending with a faceless star? My dad squeezes my shoulder. "Let's not give up yet. It could still show up."

"Sure," I say, trying to keep my voice even. The truth is, I've already given up. I know I will never see that mask again.

Derek nudges me with his foot. "Why don't you just order another costume?"

I stare at him. It takes a moment for the words to sink in. Could it really be that easy? Just like that, my little brother has come up with a brilliant solution! "Derek, you're a genius!" I shout.

My dad laughs. "Why didn't I think of that?"

"Because I'm smarter than you," Derek jokes.

Then, I remember—I've spent all my money, every last dime. "I don't have enough money for another costume," I groan. "It's all gone."

If only I hadn't rented that tuxedo! I look at Dad. He and

Mom are like a cross between a charity, a boss, and a bank. Sometimes they give out goodwill donations, sometimes they pay our salary, called allowance, and sometimes they hand out loans, which have to be repaid. I hold my breath. I'm hoping for a donation, but I'll settle for a loan.

"Let's talk to your mom when we get back," my dad says. "Maybe we can figure something out."

I let out a huge sigh of relief. If I order right away, I should have the costume in a week. I might still be able to finish my film in time for the festival. I just need to add a few more chase scenes to make it long enough for a feature-length movie.

My parents confer and announce they'll pay for half the new suit and give me a loan for the rest. I jump up and give them big hugs and then I run to the computer in my dad's office. Derek and my parents join me and my dad takes out his credit card. I find the Web site, WearTheHorror.com, and quickly track down my costume. It will be great to have a brand-new one. Even though I cleaned the old suit, a sour odor still clings to it. I click to order and a small red blurb pops up. ON BACK ORDER. APPROX. 6 WEEKS DELIVERY. I stare at the words like they're part of a tricky math equation. Really tricky, like unsolvable.

"Oh, no," my mother murmurs. "They're all sold out."

"How can they be sold out?" I cry. "It's April! Halloween is six months away! Who would order a slug costume at this time of year, except me?"

“Maybe someone else is making a movie about a giant slug,” Derek pipes up.

“I’m pretty sure I’m the only one dumb enough to be making a mollusk movie,” I mutter.

“They probably don’t keep many in stock right now,” my dad says. “Try another Web site.”

We find the costume on three more sites, and they all say ON BACK ORDER.

“They probably come all the way from China,” Derek says. “Everything comes from China. Maybe they had a fire in the factory or maybe the workers went on strike. Maybe you could shoot a scene where someone cuts off his head and gallons of slime spew out, like a geyser! That would be a great end to your movie!”

I cover my ears with my hands. I know Derek is trying to help, but if he babbles anymore I’m going to scream. The lump reappears in my throat, so big I feel like it’s choking me. In another minute, all the spit I can’t swallow is going to back up and overflow out my eyes.

“There’s got to be something we can do,” my mother says.

I shake my head, push back from the desk, and run upstairs. My life is officially a big mess. After I throw myself on the bed, Wilma tries to lick my face. I guess she’s trying to comfort me. Either that, or my tears taste good. All the scenes we’ve shot run through my mind—the wedding, the fight scene, the flying saucer, even Leo's footage. It's all useless now. The award just disappeared along with my slug mask. I won't be able to prove to Tristan that I know what I'm doing. His movie will probably win. He will get his picture in the newspaper and I will be a has-been movie director at the age of twelve. Even worse, I know it's my fault. I should have checked on the mask. I never should have asked Leo to be in my movie.

Somebody knocks softly at my door. "Kate?" It's my mother.

Part of me wants to cry all by myself, with Wilma lapping up the tears. Another bigger part of me wants my mom to wrap her arms around me. I wipe my eyes and hunch on a corner of the bed. "Come in."

The door cracks open and my mother sits down next to me. She brushes the hair back from my face. "Hey, your dad and I were thinking. Why don't you put this movie on hold until you get a new mask? You can enter it in the festival next year. In the meantime, you can start something else for fun...."

"I can't!" I burst out. "I have to enter it this year or Tristan's going to win the prize!"

My mother looks confused. "Who is Tristan?"

"A new kid at school. He moved here from New York City. He's making a movie, too, and it's probably way better than mine. He's been making fun of my movie and telling everyone he's going to win. There's no point in even finishing mine," I add gloomily, "since it won't be in time for the film festival."

My mother puts an arm around my shoulders. "Kate, I think it's wonderful that you want to take part in the festival, but since when did that become the whole reason for making your movie?" She gives me one of those deep, gaze-into-your-soul, Mom looks. "You've always made movies because it's what you like to do. Because it's fun."

"It's all about the festivals!" I break in. "You have to get your film accepted if you want to be somebody! You have to meet people and win awards."

I stop short and take a deep breath. I also need to win in order to impress my classmates. When you're a seventh grader with bullies dogging your footsteps, and you can't sing and dance, and you don't do sports, you need some way to rise to the top and get noticed. If I can wave that award under Tristan's nose, maybe he'll go back to the Crunched-up Apple where he belongs.

Lizzy plays soccer. Alyssa is on the volleyball team. Margaret is in Drama and Doris does math problems. They all have normal hobbies. Well, Doris is skewed to the far weird side of normal but she's a genius, so that's okay. I don't do any of that stuff. For some reason, I just love to make movies. I love the feeling of framing a shot and figuring out props and making body fluids, and then finally putting it all together in a story with sound and pictures and music and cool special effects.

My mother is giving me a funny look. "Who says you have to do all this?"

"Tristan," I mutter.

"Well, maybe that's why he makes movies. You've always done it because you love it. And if you do what you love, sooner or later you'll get recognized. Even if you don't, at least you're doing what you enjoy. It's supposed to be fun, remember?"

I nod, wiping my nose. My mother hands me a tissue. It's true, I've been too worried to enjoy this movie very much. It feels more like a huge homework assignment, where I have to get an A+ just to pass.

My mother hugs me and I cling to her for a moment. She pushes the hair out of my eyes and smiles. "Anybody in there?"

Instead of rolling my eyes like I usually do, I just smile back. I think sometimes it's okay to pretend you're only ten, when no one else is looking.

"Think about what I said, okay?"

I nod. She kisses me on the forehead and leaves. I take a deep, shaky breath. Maybe I have been taking this whole movie thing a little too seriously.

There's another tap on my door. It's Derek, carrying a black canvas bag. I quickly rub the tears out of my eyes. He stares around my room and finally perches next to me on the bed. "Sorry about your movie."

"Thanks."

There's a long awkward pause. I try to think of a polite way to ask him to leave, when he suddenly pushes the bag toward me. "Here. I decided you can use my spy gear for another week." He stares at his toes. "It's on the house."

"Derek, you're the best!" I sling an arm over his shoulders and hug him, then rub my knuckles on his head.

"Ouch!" he shouts. "No hugs, no kisses! And it's only for one week, so make sure you nail it this time."

"Oh, I will," I tell him.

Bride of Slug Man has gone down in flames, but *Belly of the Naked Bully* is about to rise from the ashes. Except for the naked part. My movies are strictly PG-13.

First thing Monday morning, I reinstall the camera in Margaret's locker and give Doris the wristwatch. Still, a shroud of gloom hangs over us. Everyone is sure they saw the mask but no one can remember what happened to it. Our gloom deepens as the days tick by and Paul and Blake refuse to cooperate. In desperation, I start wearing the spy sunglasses outside before and after school, even though they raise my nerd factor to dangerously high levels. Margaret dawdles at her locker before every class. Nothing works. Paul and Blake still make our lives miserable, just not on camera.

On Friday, Noah stops by my locker between classes and asks if I've found the mask. When I give him the bad news, he groans and clutches his head.

"I wish I could remember what happened, Kate! I know I took it off after Leo let go of me. I must have thrown it down on the ground." He rubs his eyes, grinding his palms into his sockets until I want to grab his wrists and yank them away. When he finally drops his hands, I'm surprised his eyeballs aren't liquefied. "I don't know what I did with it," he babbles. "I've been trying to remember and Doris thinks it's all my fault...."

"What?" I say sharply. "Doris is blaming you?"

"Well, yeah." He stuffs his hands in his pockets. "She's probably right. I was wearing the mask."

"Noah, it wasn't your fault. You just had your brains rattled by an old, drunk guy. I don't blame you for not remembering."

Noah's whole body convulses in a major sigh of relief. "Really? Because Doris said—"

"Forget what Doris said," I cut in. I need to have a talk with that girl.

"Do you think..." Noah starts, then blushes.

I'm pretty sure I already know the question. I just don't know the answer. "What is it, Noah?"

"Nothing," he mumbles.

"Is it about Doris?" I ask helpfully.

Noah nods, his Adam's apple bouncing. He grins painfully at something over my shoulder. It looks like I'm going to have to do all the heavy lifting here.

"Noah, are you wondering if Doris likes you?"

His face turns bright red and his eyes bounce off the walls and land on me. His smile changes, grows shyer. Bingo.

"No," he says. "No, that's not it."

I feel like groaning. I've never seen two people who liked each other so much who were so clueless how to show it.

"That's too bad," I say casually, "because I was just talking about you with her."

We did talk about him once, a week ago. Compared to the entire gazillion-year history of the universe, that counts as *just*.

Noah practically sputters in excitement. "Really, what did she say? Does she, you know, do you think she . . . ?" He can't bring himself to finish the question.

I shrug cagily. "You first, Noah. Do you like Doris?"

He tries to lean smoothly against the locker but it's farther away than he thinks and his long body ends up at an awkward angle. He folds his arms, trying to make it work. "I don't know. Sure. Why wouldn't I? She's pretty smart."

"*Pretty* smart?" I say.

Noah giggles. "Yeah, really smart."

"I don't mean do you like her. I mean, do you *like* her?"

Noah looks like he might make a run for it. I'm starting to see why Doris is so severe with him. I lean forward and frown. "Noah, look at me."

His eyes bounce to me. He does have nice eyes, when they actually stay focused for a moment.

"Okay." He expels a huge breath of air. "Yeah, I kind of like Doris. Does she like me?"

"Well . . ." I say.

Just then, I hear my name. It's Margaret, waving to us. "Hi guys!" She hurries over and I can tell she's dying to know what we're talking about.

Noah ducks his head and stammers, "Hi . . . hello. . . ." He grins at the wall. "I guess I should get to class."

This whole matchmaking business is a lot harder than it looks.

"What is this, a meeting of the Dork Club?" a voice booms behind us.

I cringe at the sound. Paul Corbett. He and Blake stroll over, grinning. Paul pokes Noah in the chest with his finger.

"If it isn't Nose Phlegm hanging out with the nerd herd."

Nerd herd? He must have heard that on TV. Paul isn't nearly clever enough to come up with it on his own.

"Say, Phlegmy, I've got a great idea. Let's see if you can get inside Crapkate's locker. I'll bet you can fit if you squeeze in really tight."

Trust Paul to come up with such a stupid idea. Only a human accordion could fold himself into such a tiny space. As I stare at my skinny, messy locker, I notice Derek's sunglasses perched on the top shelf. Of course! This is it. I just need to act casual. Hopefully it won't seem too strange that I'm putting on sunglasses indoors. As I reach for them, Paul sticks out his hand and takes them.

"These are the dorkiest sunglasses I've ever seen."

He tosses them to Blake. With my razor-sharp reflexes, honed in epic battles of dodgeball, I snag them in midair. Blake tries to grab them from me but I'm way too fast. I flick the ON button as I'm putting them on.

"Those look retarded," Paul informs me. "You look even stupider than normal."

"That's not nice, Paul," I say sweetly. "And stupider isn't a word."

He glares at me and then turns his attention back to Noah. "Okay, nose snot, I'll give you a choice." Paul pulls out his black marker. I'll bet he carries it just so he can draw on people. He waves it in Noah's face. "You can either climb into the locker, or I'll draw a mustache on your face. Which sounds like more fun?"

Blake snickers. "Do both."

"I've got to get to class," Noah mumbles.

"We all do," Margaret pipes up. "We're going to be late."

Paul grins. "Mustache it is, then."

Blake grabs Noah and Paul reaches up to draw on his face. Poor Noah struggles, but not really. He knows if he fights back too hard, he'll just end up getting hurt. A little voice in my head says this is exactly the footage we need. It doesn't seem fair that Noah is the victim, though. He didn't sign on for this spy mission. And how can he show his face to Doris with a Magic Marker mustache on it? Call me a romantic, but I can't let him endure the humiliation. At the last moment, I lunge forward and grab the marker out of Paul's hand. "Stop it, Paul!"

As Paul swings around to take it back, his face collides with the marker, leaving a black gash on his cheek. Okay, clearly I should have thought this through a little more.

"She got you, man!" Blake crows.

He thinks the black mark is hilarious. Paul, not so much. He grabs the marker from me and pushes me hard against the lockers, his face a furious red. When Paul Corbett gets really mad, he gets really crazy. He's already been suspended once for fighting this year.

"You want to draw on faces?" Paul yells.

"I didn't draw on you," I point out. "It was an accident."

Paul isn't interested in minor details. He shakes me and my head bangs back against the locker. That hurt. The sunglasses slide off my face. I manage to catch them but Paul hits them out of my hand and they clatter to the ground. Margaret tries to grab Paul's arm before he draws on my face, but Blake blocks her.

"Leave her alone!" Noah blurts. It doesn't sound convincing but at least he's trying.

"Get my sunglasses!" I tell Margaret.

She dives down but Paul gets there first. He steps on them with his big clodhopper shoe and I hear the horrible crunch of plastic. It's all happened so quickly, I can't even think straight. All I know is, my brother's spy shades are destroyed, and along with them our best evidence to nail

Paul and Blake. And there's not a teacher in sight. Aren't they supposed to patrol the hallways? They're probably all camped out in the teacher's lounge, gulping down coffee and doughnuts. I shove back hard against Paul but he's gripping me too tightly.

"Oops, were those your ugly sunglasses? I just did you a favor." He holds the marker over my face. "How about a mustache and a beard, Crapkate? That should improve your looks."

"What's going on?"

The voice seems to come out of nowhere. We all pause, look around. There stands Tristan Kingsley, of all people. He looks curiously at Paul and Blake. "What are you guys doing?"

"Hey, Kingsley," Paul says. "Just in time. I'm giving Crapkate a face tattoo. Wanna help?" He holds the marker out to Tristan.

"Crapkate?" Tristan's eyes flick to me like he's putting two and two together, figuring out that's my nickname. A horrible dread clutches my chest. Here I am, shoved against a locker, Paul Corbett grabbing me with his Neanderthal fists, other students watching with pity, and Tristan is about to make my humiliation complete by writing on my face.

Tristan eyes the marker, then shrugs. "Nah. You should let her go."

"I'm just paying her back for this." Paul shows him the mark on his cheek.

"That was an accident," I say. "He was trying to draw on Noah's face."

Tristan sighs. "Come on, man, let her go. It's time for class."

The problem is, he's new. He doesn't really know Paul and Blake. Still, they're in his movie. They're friends. Maybe that means they'll listen to him and back down.

Paul shrugs. "Then be a baby and run along to class. Whatever."

"Let her go, Paul," Tristan says more firmly. He doesn't sound nervous, which he should be.

"Are you gonna make me?" Paul fires back. He doesn't like to be told what to do.

Tristan rolls his eyes. "Dude, are you still in grade school?"

Paul's eyes narrow. He also doesn't take criticism well. He pushes me one last time and steps toward Tristan. I know this isn't going to end well because it's two to one and Tristan is smaller than both of them. I quickly duck down and pick up the sunglasses. One of the lenses is cracked. Paul moves to push Tristan, but Tristan pulls some kind of fast maneuver and Paul ends up on the floor, looking surprised. Blake lurches forward but the same thing happens. Blake, on the floor, dazed. By this time, kids have circled around and are calling out names. "Come on, Kingsley, nail 'em!" "Finish it, Corbett!"

Paul tries a tackle but Tristan delivers a kick to his stomach that stops him cold. Blake grabs Tristan from behind and Paul jumps up looking ready to tear his head off. Tristan's good luck just ended. Or maybe not, because the noise has finally brought a teacher into the hallway. Mr. Brumberg charges into the circle. "What is going on here?" he thunders, even though it's obviously a fight. All three boys put on an innocent face. Blake grudgingly lets go of Tristan.

"Just working out a fight scene for my movie," Tristan explains. "Sorry; didn't mean to get so loud."

"Everyone move along," Mr. Brumberg barks. "You're all going to be late for class."

Paul points a finger at Tristan, like *just wait*, and slouches away. Noah mumbles thanks and hurries off, looking embarrassed and relieved.

"Thank you so much, Tristan," Margaret gushes. "How did you do that?"

"*Why* would you do that?" I blurt. I know it doesn't sound exactly grateful, but it's what popped into my head. Why would a small guy take on two big guys in a fight that doesn't concern him?

Tristan shrugs. "I have two little sisters. I guess it's a habit."

"But how did you do it?" Margaret is still gushing. "You made it look so easy!"

Another modest shrug. "I took karate in New York."

"Karate!" Margaret exudes enough admiration for the both of us.

"Thanks," I mutter.

I wish I could just scrunch myself into my locker and shut the door. Why did Tristan, of all people, have to see me getting shoved around? When we first met, he thought I was cool. Now he knows my nickname. He knows I get picked on. He probably feels embarrassed for me. Even worse, maybe he feels sorry for me.

"Hey, I heard what happened with your movie," he says.

Bad news travels faster than a speeding bullet at our school. Mr. Brumberg steps forward and cuts Tristan short. "Off to class. All of you."

I grab Margaret's arm. "We're going to be late." As we run down the hall, she chatters on about how brave Tristan was. I listen glumly because there's nothing more annoying than being rescued by someone you dislike.

20

I can't pay attention in math class. I keep fingering the broken sunglasses in my pocket. Derek will go ballistic when he sees them. My movie is back-burnered, my budget is busted, and now I have to buy a new pair of expensive spy shades. And I just filmed an amazing sequence, like something out of a TV reality show—*Dork Dynasty*, complete with fighting and insults and a so-called hero to save the day. It doesn't matter, though, because the digital file is probably ruined. I heave a deep sigh. It seems like Henrietta and I are soul mates.

There is a tiny chance, about the size of an octopus's eye, that the sunglasses could still work. At the end of the day, I rush to my locker to get Derek's tablet. I'm showing the crumpled shades to Alyssa and Lizzy when Margaret and Doris hurry over.

"You were lucky Tristan came along," Doris observes.

"Tristan?" Alyssa and Lizzy echo together. I guess I forgot to mention that he showed up.

"He beat up Paul *and* Blake," Margaret tells them.

"He didn't beat them up," I interrupt. "He just . . . got lucky."

"Too bad Noah didn't do anything," Doris says in a sour voice.

There she goes again, bad-mouthing Noah. Enough is enough. I turn to her. "Doris, why are you acting so mean to Noah? What did he do?"

Doris pulls her sour pickle face. "I'm not mean to him. He just . . . annoys me."

"But you two got along great the day of the wedding shoot," Margaret points out.

"I know," Doris flares, "and ever since then he's been following me around like a puppy dog. He used to be fun before. Now, he's just . . . sappy." Doris stares at her brown, thick-soled shoes. "And every time he walks by, you guys look at me. I see you elbowing each other. It makes me uncomfortable."

Hmm. I'm starting to get the picture. Doris likes the old, funny Noah, not this new lovesick one. And she doesn't want us treating the whole thing like we're reality show judges, making comments and cheering on our favorites. Even when it comes to romance, Doris is pretty logical.

"You know," Margaret says gently, "Noah's acting that way because he likes you."

Doris shrugs, still staring at her shoes.

Lizzy pops her gum. "You want one of us to talk to him?"

"No!" Doris looks flustered again. "Just forget about it, okay? I don't want to talk about it."

Awkward silence. Margaret nudges me. "I can't believe Paul stepped on your sunglasses," she says in a let's-change-the-subject voice. "I wanted to step on his buttface!"

We all giggle, shocked. "Margaret! Did you really just say that?"

"I think you almost used a swear word!"

She turns pink. "I'm not as big a wimp as you all think I am."

"Speaking of buttface," I say, "it's time to assess the damage."

We hurry to the girls' bathroom. Tina Turlick and Emily Foster are combing their hair in front of the bathroom mirror. As we walk in, I overhear Emily say something about how Tristan totally likes Lydia. It gives me a funny feeling in my stomach. Not that I care who Tristan Kingsley likes. He can like anyone he wants. It's just so predictable that he would fall for Lydia. It's like a boring Hollywood formula script, *Cute New Boy Falls for Most Popular Girl.* How many times has that been done? As soon as Tina and Emily see me, they exchange a look and stop talking.

"How's your slug movie going, Kate?" Tina asks in an overly sweet voice.

"Amazing," I say loftily.

"Shooting with Tristan was so much fun," Tina says. "Everybody was there. It was like a big party. His parents are so nice. They bought everyone pizza and ice cream at the end."

Why is it that *everyone* mentions the pizza and ice cream? We had pizza, too! Of course, it wasn't Don Bernatello's. Maybe I should have spent more of my budget on food.

"Tristan is so going to win the student prize at the festival. He totally knows he's got it locked up." Emily glances at me in the mirror. "I mean, you could win it too, Kate." Her voice makes it clear that she doesn't think I have a chance. So now Tristan is bragging about the festival prize! I may obsess about winning, but at least I don't say it out loud.

I shrug like it's no big deal. Alyssa, Margaret, and I whip out combs and press in toward the mirror, crowding them. Doris gapes at us. I don't think she carries grooming accessories. Tina and Emily exchange a look, then grab their backpacks and hurry out. Finally, we have some privacy. Alyssa tears a sheet of paper from a notebook and writes OUT OF SERVICE. She spits the gum out of her mouth and sticks the sign on the door. The door doesn't lock, so she and Lizzy lean against it in case anyone tries to walk in.

"Okay," Alyssa says. "Let's see what you've got."

"Probably nothing," I mutter. I plug one end of the tiny cable into the sunglasses and the other into the tablet. The seconds tick by. The screen stays blank. "I knew it," I groan. "Paul broke them."

"Did you turn them on?" Doris asks.

Oops. I guess that's why Doris is a genius. Everyone gives me a hard time as I flick the switch in the back of the glasses. We hold our breath. The tiny light suddenly glows red. It's exciting, but it doesn't mean the video file survived. Once again, nothing happens. Just as I'm about to announce they're ruined, a small screen pops up on the tablet. We erupt in cheers and high fives until someone pushes against the bathroom door. We all freeze. If it's a teacher, we're going to be in Detentionville doing some serious time.

"Hey, who's in there?" somebody calls. "Open up!"

"Sounds like a sixth grader," Alyssa whispers.

Doris holds up a finger. "Cleaning in here," she shouts, in a croaky voice about two shades lower than normal. "Go upstairs!"

We hear a muffled groan and then footsteps hurry away. The moment of truth is at hand. I take a deep breath and press PLAY.

Suddenly, there's Paul's grinning face telling me my

sunglasses look retarded. What's amazing is the quality, considering it's a tiny camera in a cheap plastic pair of sunglasses. His voice comes across loud and clear as he orders Noah to climb into my locker. We watch as Blake grabs Noah and Paul tries to draw on his face. My own voice sounds funny, way too high, as I shout at him to stop it. Is that really how I sound, like Alvin the Chipmunk's older sister? The video suddenly gets shaky.

"You were moving your head too much," Alyssa helpfully informs me.

"I was being throttled," I retort.

Still, it's clear enough when Paul slams me into the locker. The director in me kind of likes the blurred movement. It adds a cool, out-of-control vibe, like everything was happening very fast, very hectic, which I guess it was. The best part is, the sunglasses landed faceup so there's a clear shot of Paul's foot getting bigger and bigger until there's a loud crunch, and then the screen goes black.

Everybody's eyes are round and everybody's grinning. I can feel the same gleeful expression on my own face.

"Wow," Alyssa says. "I cannot believe Paul and Blake are so out of control." She shoots a thoughtful glance at Margaret. "You guys should have told us it was this bad."

It sounds strange at first, because Alyssa has watched Paul and Blake for years. I guess watching them on video makes their nastiness clearer. In real life something bad happens and then it's over. It may stay in the victim's mind but everyone else forgets about it. On video, it doesn't fade away because you can replay it over and over, which we do, three more times.

Lizzy gives me a high five. "It's unbelievable!"

"Kate, it's a masterpiece." Margaret's voice is quiet, almost reverent. "And it was all your idea."

"It is kind of epic," I modestly agree.

"No, no." Margaret stares seriously around at us. "It's a *masterpiece*. Do you know why?" She shakes her head like she still can't believe it. "Not only did we record them both acting like jerks, but Paul shoves you against the lockers. That's beyond bullying. That's like, almost as bad as hitting you. *And* he destroys your property on purpose. We actually got them. We got them."

Margaret is getting all worked up. She goes quiet, her lower lip trembling. Her eyes turn red and she turns away to wipe them. "Sorry," she mutters. "I'm just being silly."

I immediately go all don't-know-what-to-do awkward because I'm sort of stunned. All this time, I never knew the bullying bothered her *this* much. I should have known. Isn't that what friends are for? But she was always so good at hiding it. Margaret is so noble that she even tried to make excuses for Paul's and Blake's behavior in the past. If they hadn't started bullying me, would I ever have come to her rescue? I hesitate, feeling guilty, wondering what to do.

Doris is even more clueless than I am. She's staring at Margaret with her mouth open, probably trying to figure out the square root of happy tears. Lizzy coos an unhelpful "awwww..." and shoots a look my way like, *Do something!* It's Alyssa who knows just the right thing to do. She swoops forward and gives Margaret a big hug, then looks her in the eye. "Those guys so deserve this," she says quietly. "You know that better than anyone, Margaret. We should have done this for you a long time ago."

My thoughts exactly. I'm glad Alyssa said it, though. Margaret and Alyssa share one of those girly, happy smiles together and I smile too, because I know at last they're truly friends now, and not just because of me.

I have plenty of time to think about everything that's happened on the bus ride home. Lizzy sits next to me but she's listening to music with her earbuds while she does homework. That's okay because I don't feel like talking. My stomach feels queasy as I think about the fight with Paul and Blake. I like to think I'm pretty tough but I guess I'm not. Maybe I need to take up weight lifting. Still, when I remember the great footage we got, I feel pumped up, like I just aced a bodybuilding session. Those two are so busted! I grin, imagining Paul's face as he watches himself acting like an idiot. Still, what if he doesn't care? What if nothing changes? My stomach goes back to queasy.

And then there's Tristan. Nobody gets on Paul's and Blake's bad side if they can help it. Besides, they're in his movie, and Tristan called my movie retarded. So why did he stick up for Margaret and me? It doesn't make sense. I picture Tristan sitting around at lunch with Paul and Blake, making jokes about me. Then, it occurs to me. I've never seen them eat lunch together or even hang out after school, unless they're in a group. After today's fight, it seems they must not be very good friends after all. What if Tristan never made fun of *Bride of Slug Man*? What if Paul made it all up just to annoy me? And what if it was Paul's brilliant idea to steal people from my sign-up sheet, and Tristan never knew about it?

In movies, you can usually tell the good guys from the bad guys, but not always. Like in Harry Potter, one of the villains turns out to be a hero. In a book or movie, that's a great plot twist. In real life, not knowing can keep you awake at night. I'm not moving Tristan into the hero column yet, but maybe he doesn't belong with Voldemort, either. I graze on my nails, trying to puzzle him out. As kids clear off the bus, the noise quiets. Suddenly, I hear Tristan's voice. I furtively glance over my shoulder. Olivia Sykes and Jennifer Adams are both sitting behind him, leaning forward in their seats to see what he's working on.

"They're called storyboards," he tells them. "For a scene in my movie. It helps me figure out how I'm going to shoot it."

"That is so cool!" Olivia squeals. "I love this one!"

Jealousy snakes through me. I'm dying to see his

storyboards. Instead, I have to listen to Olivia and Jennifer complimenting them.

"Some of us are going roller-skating this Saturday," Olivia says. "You want to go with us?"

Tristan flips back his hair as he erases something on his board. "I'm working on my movie. Thanks, though."

Olivia pouts a little. "Don't you ever get tired of working on that thing?"

Tristan glances up, surprised. "Why would I get tired of it?"

Olivia shrugs. She doesn't get it, but I do. I get it completely. That's when it hits me—this kid likes to make movies! Like, somehow I forgot that fact even though I think about Tristan and his movie every day. He has the same crazy hobby that I do! We should be friends. I cringe as I remember my Elvis explanation. I must have sounded so stuck-up. He probably doesn't even want to talk to me now. Even worse, he knows my nickname. I sigh as I turn around and stare out the window. Lizzy waves good-bye as she and Olivia get off at their stop. Jack Timner hurries past and I wonder if he's still grounded. That would make it tough for Tristan to finish his movie. Curiosity gnaws at me. Has he had many problems with his shoot? I'll bet not nearly as many as I've had. Still, it would be fun to talk to him about it. Except we're not talking.

When we reach Tristan's stop and he hurries up the aisle, three different girls call good-bye to him. I roll my eyes.

Part of me really wants him to be a Voldemort. But why? I've made this whole movie thing a competition. Maybe it doesn't have to be about beating him. Maybe the race is all in my head. If my brains had wheels, they'd be spinning in mud right now. It's so hard to figure out what's really going on. My life is as confusing as the plot of a foreign movie. One thing is crystal clear, though. As Sal grinds the gears and we chug closer and closer to my stop, my stomach graduates from queasy to full-on sick. It's Friday. Derek let me use his spy tools all week, and now he'll want them back. What can I possibly tell him? The truth, I guess. One spook to another.

Derek's elementary school had a half-day so he's already parked in front of the TV, watching cartoons, when I get home. As soon as I walk in, he jumps up. "How did it go? Did you get what you need? Where's my gear? I let you use it for two weeks!" He smiles, pleased at his own generosity. I try to smile back but it's like my lips snag on a rotten tooth. I can't quite manage it. I hand him the spy camera, the tablet, and the wristwatch. He waits for me to hand over his favorite, newest toy, the one he entrusted to my care. I can't think of any way to break the news gently. Finally, I just show Derek the crumpled sunglasses. His face gets all horrified, like he's staring at a dead corpse.

"I'll get you the money to replace them," I blurt. "By the end of the week. I swear."

"You broke them!" he yells.

"I didn't do it," I say quickly. "The perp did."

Derek's eyes are bugged out. He's about to start shrieking but, just as I'd hoped, he can't resist the bait. "The perp? Really? You blew your cover. I knew it," he scoffs. "Amateurs shouldn't mess with spying."

"Wrong. He never figured it out. It was just bad luck. The sunglasses fell during the fight and he stepped on them."

Derek's eyes go round. "You were in a *fight*? Are you in trouble? Do Mom and Dad know?"

"No, and they better not find out." I give him a look.

He grabs the glasses, offended. "I never give up classified info. Maybe under torture. I can hold out a long time, though. I'm in training." He shows me a big greenish bruise on his arm.

"What is that?"

He punches himself right on the bruise. "I've been seeing how much I can take. Look, see?" He punches himself again, wincing. "I think I'd last a while."

Normally I'd say something like, *Maybe you should let me stick your head in a toilet for practice,* but now isn't the time for sarcasm. "That is amazing!" I gush instead. "That looks so painful!"

He grins modestly and rolls his sleeve back down. "You owe me forty dollars."

"I know. Give me a week, that's all I need."

"A week!" he shouts. "I let you have this stuff for two weeks already! I'm telling Mom and Dad!"

Uh-oh. Just like I feared, he's playing the Mom and Dad card. I've got to go into grovel mode, pronto.

"Derek, please," I beg. "I'm really, really sorry but it wasn't my fault. I'm broke but I'm going to get that money even if I have to sell something of mine. Ple-e-ease."

He crosses his arms. "What would you sell?"

"I don't know. Maybe my camera."

I have no intention of selling my precious camera, but at least this lets Derek know I'm serious. He woefully checks out the ruined frames again. "You broke my spy glasses," he whines. "It's not fair. Those were mine."

"But you know what? They worked!" I pause to let this sink in. "We got the evidence we need, Derek. We busted the ring!"

"Whoa, really?" He looks impressed. "All thanks to my spy gear?"

"Your stuff is awesome," I assure him.

I never thought of Paul and Blake as a ring before, but it has a nice sound to it. They do enough damage for a whole gang.

Derek heaves a gargantuan sigh. "I can't believe I'm doing this. One week. That's it. Then I want my money."

"Thank you so much!" I try to give him a hug but he goes into a judo stance and tries to karate chop me.

"You didn't do too bad for a first-timer," he tells me. "So, you want to join my spy club?"

I almost laugh out loud but something in Derek's face

makes me stop. After all, he did let me use his gear. He even gave me an extra week. Without Derek, my friends and I wouldn't have the goods on Paul and Blake. Who knows? Maybe one day Derek *will* be a spy. He's so weird, he could end up head of the CIA. It would probably be wise to stay on his good side. And I'm a sucker for his wide-eyed *I'm your little brother with fragile self-esteem* look. It gets me every time.

I lightly punch him on his bruise and he grins and winces at the same time. "Sure," I say. "Why not?"

22

We've got the bait. Now, we need to figure out how to spring the trap. We can't agree on the best way to show Paul and Blake the video. Lizzy wants to project it on a wall for major impact, but that's not very discreet. Plus, the file size is too small. We finally decide to use a computer. But how and when? It's not like we can send them an invitation. If we try it at school, we would have to avoid teachers and other kids. Most classrooms are locked when not in use, so it would be hard to find a private spot, and even harder to lure them there. But if not at school, then where?

We debate and argue all week long. Lizzy finally provides the answer at lunch on Friday. "Twisters," she says. "Tonight. I overheard Paul and Blake talking about it. They're seeing a movie first and then going to Twisters."

We're all quiet as this sinks in. Tonight. That's in a few hours. Deep down, I didn't think we would ever actually get this far. It's like discussing the best way to grab a tiger by the tail. In the end, you just have to take a deep breath, close your eyes, and do it.

"Twisters will be really crowded," Doris says. "Other kids might see."

Margaret nods. "That's true." Are she and Doris both getting cold feet?

Lizzy bites into her slice of pizza. "It's a noisy restaurant. No one will pay any attention."

"And it's in public," I point out. "I think that's safer."

Ever since Paul banged me up against the lockers, I've decided I really don't need any more alone time with him. I'd rather spend the night in our haunted henhouse than meet him in a dark, deserted alley.

We lay our plans to meet at Twisters and spring an ambush. It shouldn't take long. The recording is a minute, tops, although they may need to see it a few times for it to sink in. Since I have a certain way with words, I'll explain exactly what we want. As in, be nice or be benched. They're not the brightest boys, but I think they'll get it.

Or will they? I glance at the next table where Blake and Paul are wolfing down their lunches. We're about to take on the two meanest boys in seventh grade. What if they just laugh in our faces? What if they don't care enough about baseball to change their ways? We'll have to follow through on our threat and show the footage to Principal Safire and Coach Morton. Even if they do get benched, we've still lost. Paul and Blake will hound us day and night and make us all miserable. This crazy plan only works if they don't want to risk getting kicked off the baseball team.

I nibble on organic cheese crisps and try to pay attention as Alyssa tells Margaret about the makeup that her mother sells. She promises to bring Margaret some lip gloss to try on. Doris is sucking down a chocolate milk, staring off into space. "And you too, Doris," Alyssa says. "You looked so pretty the day of the wedding shoot."

Doris's eyes go wide as she wipes the chocolate milk mustache off her lip. "Um, I don't know."

We all smile. At least Doris isn't rejecting the idea. For a second, I let myself enjoy this moment. It's so ordinary—just another lunch period in the cafeteria. But it's sweet, too. The jokes, the mini dramas, that comfortable sense of belonging. One day, I might look back and miss this. That's the weird thing about friendships. You can become as close as sisters. You can share your biggest secrets, things you wouldn't even tell your real sister. Then, something happens—maybe a fight, or a parent gets a job transfer. Suddenly, the friend is gone. That almost happened to Alyssa and me last semester. Friendships are kind of like chickens. You have to feed them and take care of them. Otherwise, they can get worms or parasites or fungal infections and just wither away.

I should be protecting my friends. Instead, I might be

making them victims. What if Paul and Blake start teasing Alyssa, Lizzy, and Doris? They might resent it. They might decide it was my fault. I'd rather have Paul bang my head against the lockers every day than have my friends hate me. The more I think about it, the more I realize I may be dragging everyone into a big mistake. Blake is one of those kids who just goes along, but Paul is bad news. He's got "future inmate" written all over him. They probably already have a cell reserved for him at the county jail.

I clear my throat. "I've been thinking."

Lizzy groans. "Not again."

"Ha-ha," I say loftily. "Very funny."

"I hope this isn't about another movie," Alyssa says. "I'm still combing globs of slime out of my hair."

Doris sucks loudly on her straw. "Okay, let's hear it. What is it this time?"

I take a deep breath. "I think Margaret and I should go alone to Twisters tonight."

Alyssa frowns, like she suspects I'm playing favorites. "Why shouldn't we go, too?"

"This may not go the way we want," I remind them. "Our whole plan blows apart if Paul and Blake don't care about the video. And once they've seen it, they're going to hate us. Margaret and I are already on their list, but if you guys come along, you'll be in the line of fire, too." I crumple my lunch bag. "Margaret and I can show them the video. You guys should lay low and stay out of trouble."

I'm half hoping they'll scoff at my fears. The truth is, I'd rather have them there. There's strength in numbers.

Margaret's eyes flicker from me to the others. She wipes a smudge of pizza sauce off her mouth. "That makes sense. There's no reason all of you should be targets."

"We can't let you do this by yourselves," Alyssa protests.

Lizzy nods. "We can't just abandon you."

Their words say one thing but their voices are saying another. I sense hesitation. They're worried about what might happen, too.

Doris cocks her head, thinking. "If Blake and Paul don't stop bothering you and we have to show Coach Morton the video, they'll retaliate. Things will get much worse than they are now. So the fewer of us involved, the less widespread the damage. It's logical."

Sometimes I think Doris has Vulcan blood.

"It's settled then," I say, trying to keep my voice positive.

"Perfect!" Margaret is even more cheerful than I am. She's a good actress.

"Are you sure?" Alyssa sounds relieved. "Will you guys be okay?"

"Of course." I lean back on the cafeteria stool, trying to look unworried, even as my stomach flutters. My mom has a saying she likes to throw out sometimes when Derek and I are in trouble: *You're jumping from the frying pan into the fire*. That's what it feels like. Margaret and I may be sizzling in the pan right now, but we're about to leap directly into some very hot flames.

After school, I back up the spy video to the hard drive on my computer. I wouldn't put it past those boys to grab the tablet and try to delete the file. As I'm waiting for the video to transfer, a name catches my eye. It's my *Bride of Slug Man* movie file. It gets me thinking. Maybe my first movie was just beginner's luck. Maybe I'm not serious enough to be a big Hollywood director. They probably all sit around dressed in black, drinking double espressos and chatting about French New Wave films. I'd be the only one sitting in the corner drinking a frappé, trying to figure out when the next *Star Wars* sequel is coming out. Yeah, I definitely wouldn't fit in. I guess I can't handle the strong stuff, either in movies or caffeine. And black doesn't look good on me. My favorite color is purple.

Like an old toothache coming back, Tristan's face pops into my head. I picture him on a podium in a cool, art-scene theater, accepting his award, thanking the little people, soaking up the rich film air. Dressed in black, of course.

23

After our parents drop us off at Twisters, Margaret and I hang outside for a little while. It rained earlier and the neon Twisters sign gleams red in the puddles, like spilled blood. A warm breeze riffles our hair and brings with it the rich, greasy aroma of hamburgers. My stomach growls.

"So, we'll grab a booth," I repeat, even though we both know the plan backward and forward. "When we're ready, we'll go to their table and tell them we have something to show them."

Margaret's head bobs up and down. "We play the video and explain what's going on. Shape up or else."

I grip the tablet to my chest with a sweaty hand. "Ready?"

Margaret nods and I pull open the front door. It's Friday night and the place is buzzing with voices, laughter, clinking silverware. We spot Paul and Blake in the very back, texting on their phones. Since they're together, I can't imagine who they'd be texting. Maybe their mothers. As we make our way to a booth, Paul glances up and spots us. He elbows Blake and they both smirk as we squeeze into a booth. I pretend I haven't noticed them, but my heart is thudding. We watch the video once more to make sure it's still working. Seeing it makes me feel better. I can only hope that baseball matters to them as much as they act like it does.

A sweaty, annoyed-looking waitress cruises up to our table. She probably wishes we were rich-looking adults instead of two nervous twelve-year-olds.

"Ready to order?" She whips out a pad and stares at us like we'd better be ready because this is our last chance.

"Hamburger," I say instantly. "Small Coke and fries."

"Same," Margaret says.

The waitress nods and hurries off. Margaret's face is pale. It makes her hair seem even brighter in the fluorescent light. I grab the tablet with shaking hands. "Let's get this over with."

Blake and Paul are texting again. They don't notice us until we're almost next to them. Blake stares at us, open-mouthed. Usually, we try to stay as far away from them as possible.

Paul leans back in his chair. "What do you two want?"

Margaret takes a deep breath. "We have something to show you."

Paul and Blake glance at each other, stupid grins on their faces. "Something to show us?" Paul echoes. "Like what, your ugly butt?"

I was scared before but that makes me mad. I'm fed up with Paul's trashy mouth. "Watch carefully." I hold up the tablet and hit PLAY. We watch them as they watch themselves. They grin through the whole thing like it's a clip right off *America's Funniest Home Videos*.

"Who are those good-looking dudes?" Blake jokes.

"Two dudes and three duds," Paul cracks.

That wasn't quite the reaction we were going for. My stomach feels jittery. In fact, I feel like I might lean over and puke onto their hamburgers. They can't know I'm nervous. That would ruin everything. I picture myself as a tough-talking detective in a film noir flick. "Listen up," I snap. "'Cause I'm only going to say it once. If you two morons ever bother us again, we're showing this to Coach Morton and Principal Safire."

"Like they're going to care," Paul breaks in.

"Maybe you were busy paper-bombing toilets during the last assembly," I retort. "The message was, anyone on a sports team caught bullying will be suspended from the team. Is that ringing any bells?"

"I think Coach will be interested to know one of his players is throwing girls against lockers," Margaret says. "We've got you bullying, fighting, and destroying personal property."

The cogs in their brains are slowly slipping into place. The grins slide off their faces like Jell-O jiggles sliding off a plate.

"Are you kidding?" Blake says. "Is this, like, blackmail?"

"Well, it isn't fan mail," Margaret retorts.

Paul and Blake glance at her, surprised. Her voice is quiet but she looks ready to duke it out right here and now. I'm learning that Margaret is tougher than she looks.

"That's the deal, take it or leave it," I tell them. "Leave us alone or you can kiss baseball good-bye. All you need to do is ignore us. We'll ignore you, and no one needs to ever see this video. Oh, and by the way." I reach into my pocket, pull out Derek's broken sunglasses, and slam them on the table. "You owe me forty dollars. That's part of the deal."

Paul's ears grow red and then the blood overflows into his face like a rising riptide. He balls up a napkin in one fist. I can tell baseball is doing good things for these two. They've put on some mean-looking muscle. As big as Paul has grown, Blake is even bigger. He played football last fall. I heard he was a good tackler, the kind who loves to slam other guys down hard onto the turf.

Paul throws the balled-up napkin right in my face and then leans forward and locks eyes with me. "You show that to the coach and you're dead."

"Yeah," Blake chimes in, with a little less conviction.

Paul points to the tablet. "You show it to anyone and that is nothing compared to what you're gonna get."

Okay, this is not going as planned. Just as I feared, instead of making Paul worried, we've made him mad. He stands up and towers over me, as if to make his point. I tell myself not to panic but I can feel the sweat breaking out on my face.

"What the—?" Blake is staring past us.

I turn around and there, hurrying toward us, are Alyssa, Lizzy, and Doris. Then I see they're not alone. They've brought reinforcements. Behind Doris are Noah, Nathaniel, and Trevor. Alyssa is leading the way, with a commando glint in her eye. She looks like she's heading a Navy SEAL assault team instead of a band of junior-high misfits.

She grins triumphantly as they sweep up. "You really thought we were going to let you two do this solo?" She sees me glancing at the others, my face furrowed in a question mark. "There's strength in numbers," she whispers. "Now they're going to have to deal with a lot more people than you two."

I glance at the kids behind her. They all look serious, determined even. Alyssa must have given them quite a pep talk. Or maybe they're all just really tired of being picked on.

"Okay," Alyssa says loudly. She flicks back her hair and crosses her arms. Alyssa can look pretty kick-butt when she wants to. She gives Paul a look that would shrivel the heart of a rattlesnake. "Let's show the video one more time so everyone can see how really brave Paulie-Girl and Blake-Flake are."

She hits PLAY and everybody presses in so they can watch

Paul bang me up against the lockers. The more I see it, the more pathetic it looks. Even skinny, squinty Nathaniel is shaking his head. "Wow, beating up on girls, Corbett," he sneers. "The coach will love that."

Normally, Paul would already be throwing Nathaniel in a headlock, but with all of us there, in a crowded restaurant, he doesn't know what to do. He's clenching his fists but he's starting to look uneasy. Maybe it's all finally sinking in.

Trevor nods his head. "Coach sees this and he'll stick your butts on the bench for the rest of the season." He stops and thinks about it. "Nah, he'll probably throw you right off the team."

Paul isn't going to go down without a fight. He suddenly grabs the tablet. "Thanks for the gift, Crapkate. I always wanted one of these."

I laugh out loud. "Don't you watch any movies? Nobody shows up with original files. That's a copy. And that's my dad's tablet, so you're stealing from him, not me. Does he need to call your dad?"

It's Derek's tablet, but Paul doesn't know that. His face creases and I suddenly remember that his parents are divorced and his dad moved away. He sets the tablet back down and shrugs. "Whatever. Like I'm really going to steal it. Can't you take a joke?"

Paul looks like he's out of ideas. This is it. This is the moment. He and Blake exchange a look. Which are they going to choose, bullying or baseball?

Paul drops down into his seat. "Show it to the coach," he sneers. "What do I care?" He's got a mean grin on his face like he's won, which I guess he has. He may be off the team, but now he's free to make all our lives miserable.

And right then, instead of being scared or mad, I just feel sorry for Paul. He's going to say good-bye to something he likes just so he can keep being a jerk. Even I can see it's a really bad choice.

"Satisfied, Crapkate?" He shoves the tablet at me. "Just wait until Monday morning."

We all stare at him, paralyzed. That's it, then. Our bluff didn't work. We should have known better.

"Wait a minute." Blake squints at Paul. "I don't want the coach seeing that. He'll throw us off the team."

"No, he won't," Paul scoffs. "He'll probably just yell at us and maybe bench us for a few games."

"Well, I don't want to sit out for a few games. Anyway, we could get kicked off." Blake shrugs, looking embarrassed. "If I get benched, my old man will kill me."

Blake pulls out his wallet and hands me a twenty. "Here. For the sunglasses." He tries to smile but it's more of a grimace. "Spy shades. That's pretty funny." He looks more sore than amused but at least it's a start.

Paul is shaking his head, grinning fiercely at the table as if he'd like to take a big chomp out of it. Or me. Then it hits me. Maybe he just needs a way to gracefully back down.

The waitress is waving at us. "Your food's on your table,"

she barks. "All you kids need to sit down so people can get through."

"Come on, guys. Let's go." I lean over to Margaret and murmur, "Take everyone back to the booth."

She nods and they troop away. I shove the twenty in my pocket. "Just think about it, Paul," I say quietly. "You don't need to be nice to us. Just leave us alone and we'll leave you alone, and the coach never needs to see this."

"Okay, *Crapkate*," he sneers.

"Hey," Blake says in a warning voice. "Cut it out."

"Shut up!" Paul shouts. He glares at me and I decide it's time to beat a quick retreat. Everyone is watching me at the table. I shake my head and glumly bite into my hamburger. My stomach feels hollow. Our plan came so close to working. Blake's on board but if Paul won't stop, then it was all for nothing. It's worse than nothing. We're in minus territory. We're minus any protection, with a furious ex-baseball player ready to knock our heads out of the ballpark.

I'm so nervous about going to school on Monday morning that I can't sleep Sunday night. I toss and turn in bed, staring every five minutes at the clock. It's 1:14 a.m. I shut my eyes and order myself to sleep. Paul's face swims out of the darkness, smirking. My eyes pop open. It's 1:17. What is he going to do to me at school? I'm sure he'll have something nasty planned. Dried poop in my locker? Ink in my hair? Steal my backpack? A brick-size load of dread weighs down my stomach. I flop onto my side and try counting chickens. I must doze off because when my eyes fly open, it's morning. And it's late. Really late. Either I forgot to set my alarm or I turned it off in my sleep.

I text Sal: *Don't bother*, which is our code for when I'm sick or running late, like this morning. I'm his first pickup of the day, so it saves him about twenty minutes. He can grab an extra cup of coffee before he hits the road. *Thanks kiddo*, he texts back. My mother is less happy. She delivers a lecture about responsibility while driving me to school. She'll be sorry, I think sourly to myself. Once my dead body shows up, stuffed into my locker, an inky mustache on my face, she'll wish her last words to me hadn't been a scolding.

Just as I'm stepping out of the Suburban, Paul jumps out of a red sedan in front of us. I practically dive back into the car. "Wait!" I yelp. "I think I left something!" I pretend to look for lost homework, squinting at Paul through the windshield. Something doesn't look right but it's probably just the dirty glass. My mom really should wash her car more often.

"Kate," my mother says. "What are you missing?"

"Uh, nothing," I say. "I mean, just a paper that I must have left at the house, but don't worry, it's not late."

I don't even know what I'm saying because I'm busy staring at Paul. There *is* something different about him. He has a black eye. As he slams shut the door and heads in, I see he's also got a busted lip. Paul got into a fight over the weekend. Great. He's going to be in a really awesome mood today. I've long wished that some kid would teach him a lesson, but why did it have to be this, of all weekends? I wait until he's a safe distance away, then wave good-bye to my mom and climb out. The morning hasn't even started yet and it's already a bad day. I hurry through the crowded hallway, keeping a safe distance behind Paul. Jack Timner cocks his head when he sees Paul. "Dude, what happened to you?"

Paul shoves past Jack without answering.

"Hope the other guy looks worse!" Jack calls over his shoulder.

I spin the combination on my locker, then freeze, afraid to open it. What if it's booby-trapped? I fling open the door and jump back but nothing springs out at me. So far, so good. Suddenly, someone grabs me hard by the shoulder and shakes me. I practically jump out of my skin, but it's just Alyssa. She grins as I scowl at her. "Got ya!"

"How can you be so cheerful?" I mutter. "We're all going to die today." I grab a book. "It was really brave how you guys showed up Friday night and I was glad to see you, but now you're going to regret it."

Alyssa shrugs. "Better to be in it together. There's strength in numbers."

"Yeah, if you mean the number of Paul's and Blake's biceps." I slam shut my locker and we head to class. Then, bad luck, Blake is heading right for us. The weird thing is, he's got a black eye, too, and a swollen nose. Wow, he and Paul must have gotten in a real brawl with some other kids. Maybe it happened Friday night after Twisters. Paul looked mad enough to maim somebody.

Blake is cutting a wide path as kids take one look at his face and step out of his way. And he's barreling right toward me. I actually think about turning and running the other way, but that would leave Alyssa in the lurch. Plus, he's probably a faster runner than I am. He stops short right in front of me, reaches into his pocket, and thrusts something at me. A twenty-dollar bill.

"Paul wanted me to give you this." He doesn't meet my eyes, just stares off to one side. "For the sunglasses."

"Uh, thanks." I pocket the twenty. What does it mean? Is he paying for Paul or did Paul really give him money? Then, it hits me. Maybe the fight was between these two. Maybe this twenty means that Blake won. He's got about two inches and ten pounds on Paul. Still, it must have been quite a fight.

Blake shifts from one foot to the other. "So we're good, right? You're not gonna show that to the coach?"

"That depends on Paul."

He stares straight at me. Ouch. His eye is puffy and purplish green. "Paul will leave you alone. And the others."

"Okay, that's the deal. You leave us alone, we'll leave you alone."

Blake nods. He cocks his head and squints at me like he's never gotten a good look at me before. We've known each other for years, though, ever since third grade. That was before Paul Corbett moved to town. Back then, Blake was just a big, clumsy kid who always got in trouble for squirming in his seat and shooting rubber bands at girls. Now, as he's heading away, I could swear Blake smiles the tiniest bit.

It was only for a nanosecond so I could be wrong. Maybe he was just grimacing in pain from his injuries.

"Wow," Alyssa says.

"Wow," I agree.

Nobody believes it at first. Even I don't. It's just too good to be true. I happen to be with Margaret the first time she runs into Paul in the hallway. He looks up and his eyes narrow. I brace myself but he just ducks his head and slouches off. Not a word. Margaret and I high-five each other and then we both start giggling like little girls. "We did it," she says. "We actually did it."

I guess it's time to chalk one up for the nerd herd.

The days fly by. Outside, the grass greens, tulips and daffodils pop up, and the tree branches swell with new leaves. Inside school, it feels like spring, too. Our fear has thawed and hope is sticking out its tiny buds. Paul and Blake aren't friendly, but they leave us alone. That was all we ever wanted.

The deadline for the film festival is coming up quickly. I still watch Tristan from the corner of my eye at school. I was so certain he was trying to boot me out of the way and take my place. Now, I'm not so sure. I avoid him more out of habit. After all, he could still be a Voldemort. So when he slides into the seat next to me at lunch one day, I practically go into shock. It's Alyssa's seat, but she's off buying ice cream. Right away, everyone goes silent as Margaret, Doris, and Lizzy all try not to stare.

Tristan leans back against the table. "Sorry about your movie. I heard what happened."

"Um, thanks."

"You can't get another mask?"

"No, they're sold out."

I grab my organic fruit juice and suck hard on the straw. My friends are brightly chattering now, but I know they're hanging on our every word. Maybe that's why I'm suddenly so nervous. I spot Alyssa dawdling at the end of the table with her ice cream, talking to Olivia, shooting glances our way. She catches my eye and gives me a look, but it's hard to read. It could mean, *I can't believe you're talking to that guy,* or something more positive, like *Tristan Kingsley is talking to you!* Or even, *How long do I have to stand here while you two blab?* It's hard to tell from this distance.

"So, I was wondering," Tristan says, "if you want to come and help with a big scene I'm shooting? I could use someone who knows what they're doing."

He casually reaches over, grabs one of my baked potato chips, and pops it in his mouth, then smiles at me. My brain freezes and it feels like my pupils have turned into spinning beach balls of death. Is he making fun of me? It's hard to tell. Lizzy is giving me "the look" from across the table, eyes wide, like, *Don't you dare say no.* But why would he invite me? Does he feel sorry for me? Is he mad about the whole

Elvis thing? Maybe this is his way of getting back at me. I'll show up at the shoot location and no one will be there.

"Thanks, but I think I'm busy that day." I suck on my juice until it's empty.

Tristan frowns. "I haven't told you the day yet."

Dang. My brain needs a reboot. "I figured it was this Saturday," I mutter.

He glances away. Is he disappointed? Angry? Why would Tristan Kingsley care if I show up at his shoot or not? I open my mouth to say something but it isn't words that come out. I must have sucked in a bunch of air with all that juice because it happens so fast I can't stop it—a big projectile burp, loud and hard and nasty.

From the corner of my eye, I see Margaret, Doris, and Lizzy, all bug-eyed, trying not to laugh. I'm so embarrassed that I'm paralyzed, except for the blood rushing into my face.

"Excuse me," I mumble.

Tristan is staring at me like I'm an alien life-form. Hasn't he ever heard a girl burp before? I thought he said he had sisters. I guess no one belches in the Kingsley household. I have a sudden wild desire to burst into tears. Either that, or flames. It happens, you know. It's called spontaneous combustion, when people suddenly catch on fire for no reason. My face is so hot it feels like I might go up in a whooshing blaze.

Suddenly, Tristan lets loose with an even bigger, badder belch than mine. His lips twitch into a smile and then he stands up. "You're right; the shoot is on Saturday. If you change your mind, let me know."

As soon as he strolls off, Alyssa rushes over and wants to know every word that was uttered. Margaret is laughing so hard that her glasses steam up. "Kate, what was that?"

"What?" Alyssa screeches. "What happened?"

Lizzy points at me. "Kate was talking to Tristan and she let loose with this humongous burp!"

"That was not a burp," Doris says dryly. "It was major jet propulsion."

Alyssa's eyes go round. "Seriously?"

"It was an accident!" I protest. "I didn't mean to. It just came out."

Alyssa sinks into her seat. "What did Tristan do?"

"He burped back!" Margaret grins at me. "I think that means he likes you."

Lizzy nods. "It's like a new kind of mating call."

"Ha-ha," I mutter. "Very funny. He was just trying to outdo me, as always."

Even if I was thinking about going to his shoot before, there's no way I could now. Why do these things always happen to me? I grab my juice box and crumple it in my fist.

"Why did you say you were busy?" Lizzy asks. "You should go!"

"Yeah, right. After I just burped in his face? He's probably telling all the guys and laughing about it right now. Anyway, he doesn't really mean it." I know I'm about to get a lecture from all of them so I stand up and pitch my juice box at the trash, a definite three-pointer if it goes in. It hits the rim, bounces back, and falls right at the feet of Lunch Lady. She glares at me.

"Don't throw your garbage," she barks. "Come pick this up!"

For once, I'm glad to have Lunch Lady telling me what to do. I slide out of my seat. She's standing arms on hips, like I've just committed a world-class felony. She doesn't move an inch even though the box is right at her feet. Wow, Lunch Lady has some seriously swollen ankles. And a lot of bulging purple veins. I avert my eyes, pick up the box, and throw it in the trash.

At dinner that night, I'm still thinking about Tristan's belch. It's like no matter what I do, he has to do it better. That kid is so competitive.

"What?" Derek suddenly says. "What are you staring at?"

I blink hazily, only barely catching what he said. "Huh?"

"You're staring at me!" he practically shouts.

My thoughts were so far away, I feel like I'm in a fog as I try to snap back. "Jeez, Derek, chillax. I wasn't staring at you. I was thinking about something."

My father glances at me. "What are you thinking about so hard?"

"Nothing. Just... homework." I can hardly say I was thinking about a boy who burped in my face, right?

"I'm sure your teachers would be pleased to hear you're devoting so much energy to thinking about homework," my mother says dryly. "Is everything okay at school?"

"Everything's fine," I reply a little too quickly, keeping my head down.

From the corner of my eye I see my parents exchange a glance. Dang. I was trying to fly low, but now I've popped up as a troubling blip on their radar screen. That means I should expect a reconnaissance mission to investigate. Sure enough, after dinner my dad knocks on my door and sits on my bed. "Hey Katie-did, mind if I sit down?"

My dad hardly ever uses my little-girl nickname anymore because, when I was ten, I informed him I was way too old for that. Every now and then he trots it out, I guess to remind both of us that I'm still his little girl.

"You already are sitting down," I point out. I perch next to him. I do miss the days when he would curl his big arms around me and I would practically disappear inside them. He would growl in my ear and his tickly breath always made me laugh. Now, he reaches out and tousles my hair, like he wants to hug me but isn't sure how to make it work. Even though a hug from my dad suddenly seems like a nice idea, I say, "Dad, you're messing up my hair." The sad thing is, even if my dad did put his arms around me, I wouldn't disappear anymore. I've grown way too big, even though we both like to pretend sometimes that I haven't.

"Hair crisis," he jokes. "Alert the National Guard."

I grin, rolling my eyes. "What's up?"

"That's what I was going to ask you. You've seemed kind of quiet lately. Anything going on?"

"Well, I did lose the mask to my costume, which ruined my chances of entering the film festival," I remind him.

"Right." My dad scratches his nose. "And I know that's a big deal. But I meant besides that."

I gaze at my fingernails. There is a question I'm burning to ask him but I don't know how. It's not something I would ask my mom, but my dad is kind of an expert in this area. I weigh the embarrassment factor against my need to know. "What does it mean when a boy burps in front of you?" I finally blurt.

My dad looks taken aback. He does it in front of my mom, though. She'll laugh and scold him at the same time.

"Uh, what does it mean? I guess it depends on things like when and how."

"Well, I burped first, by accident." My face feels warm just thinking about it. "We were talking and . . ."

"What were you talking about?"

"Does it really matter?"

"It might. I mean, were you joking, or was it a serious conversation? It all depends."

I sigh. "He's making a movie and he invited me to help out on it. So, anyway," I hurry on, "I was just wondering if maybe he did it to make fun of me. You know, to rub it in. Like, this is how stupid you sounded. Or maybe it's because he's so competitive. He's always trying to be better than me at everything. Like his movie, and now burping."

My dad frowns thoughtfully. "Could be those. Or maybe he's just being a gentleman."

I hoot. "A gentleman, Dad? He burped in my face!"

"Maybe he was trying to make you feel less embarrassed. I'm guessing you were embarrassed, right?"

"Completely." I pluck at a loose thread on my bedspread. "You think he noticed?"

My dad leans back, smiling. "By seventh grade, guys have a pretty good idea about what embarrasses girls."

I think about Paul and Blake and their nasty comments. Yeah, even those two have it figured out.

"I don't know this boy so I can't say for sure, but maybe he was just trying to be nice." My dad slaps me on the knee. "Is that helpful?"

"Yeah, I guess so."

"Are you going to help with his movie?"

"No," I say quickly. "No way."

My dad stands up and then stares down at his hands. "It's up to you. But a lot of people have helped you with your movies, Kate. You know better than anyone how much work it is. Maybe you should return the favor. You don't always have to be the director."

Yes, I do, I think to myself as he leaves, but even I know that's silly. Do I really always have to be in charge? I wander over to my mirror, pick up my comb, and stare at myself.

Maybe I do like to call the shots a little too much. Like Margaret trying to help during the wedding scene. It's not like it was a real movie set. I could have let her call *cut*. It wouldn't have been the end of the world.

I think back to the first day Tristan and I met. Sure, he was trying to impress everyone with his talk about French directors. But he was a new student, surrounded by kids he didn't know. I might have done the same thing in his shoes. At least Tristan had a reason for showing off. What was my excuse? I wanted to be the film guru. I wanted to take the cute new boy under my wing and show him how much I knew. I was trying to act the big Hollywood director but the only part I got right was the big Hollywood ego. Maybe acting like I know everything isn't the best way to get people to notice me. There's such a thing as getting noticed in a bad way. Like Blake and Paul. They get plenty of attention, but neither one is exactly Mr. Popular.

I could probably learn a few things from Tristan. It might even be fun. I can stay mad or I can help him finish his movie. After all, one of us should enter that film festival and it's obviously not going to be me. Maybe it'll even turn out that I do know a few things he doesn't know. Not that it matters. But it would be nice.

The next day, I spot Tristan at his locker. For once, he's alone. I veer over, hoping he might notice me and say hi first. He's digging through a huge mess at the bottom of his locker. His back is to me, which means I either have to speak up or keep moving. I decide to play it safe and walk by, but it's like my mouth didn't get the memo because it suddenly blurts, "Hey!"

Tristan glances around and smiles. "Hey."

He's sifting through balled-up papers, sweatshirts, basketball shoes. The Joker from the Batman movie leers at me from a postcard taped to the back wall.

"Your locker is an even bigger mess than mine," I say, trying to sound casual.

He stands up and scratches his head. "Yeah, it's like quicksand. My homework keeps sinking down and disappearing."

"Maybe you've got homework-eating parasites," I joke, then wince. That probably sounded really stupid.

Tristan just grins and says, "Sounds like a plot for a movie."

"How's your movie going?"

He shuts his locker door and leans against it, hands in pockets. His blond hair falls down over one eye again. I feel a sudden desire to reach forward and push it back.

"It's going good."

"How are your actors doing?" I ask slyly.

He grins ruefully and stares up at the ceiling. We both laugh. "No, they're okay, really," he says. "I mean, I just have to remind myself I'm not in New York anymore. I had some friends who went to a performing arts school there. They used to hook me up with some pretty good actors."

He says it wistfully, and it hits me that he probably wishes he were still in New York. It must have been hard to move from a huge city to a midwestern suburb.

"Do you miss it?"

"A lot." He shrugs. "Maybe I'll go to college there."

"You probably hate it here." For some reason, it makes me sad that he wishes he hadn't moved to Medford.

"I don't hate it. Some things are better. Less traffic, less noise, less dirt. People are nice, for the most part." He shoots me a look and I feel my face grow red. I guess I've been pretty unfriendly, avoiding him and trying to sound smarter than him. It's time to get out of here.

"So, about tomorrow," I say in a rush, before I chicken out. "I was going to stop by. Where are you shooting?"

"Well, it was going to be in Granger Park but now it's supposed to rain. I might have to postpone. I need a big, open space, something kind of rough, you know?"

"We have a barn," I say without thinking. Right away, I want to kick myself. The last thing I want is for Tristan to see our old, ramshackle farmhouse with the 1970s shag carpeting and the scary basement. Next to his big home in Deer Hollow, ours looks like it belongs on a TV reality show about haunted houses that need makeovers.

Tristan's eyes light up. "A barn! That would be so perfect! Do you think your parents would mind if we shot at your house tomorrow?"

I could say no and blame it on my parents. I'll avoid all

those nosy kids snooping around my house. I look straight into Tristan's blue eyes and crumble. "I'm sure they won't mind at all!"

Tristan is nodding and smiling but there's a train whistle going off somewhere in the back of my head, making it hard to hear. He and his entire cast of friends are coming to my house. Tomorrow. I take a step backward. Entrances and exits are always tricky. Right now, faster is better. I take off like a shot and call over my shoulder, "I'll text you my address!"

I heard that Paul and Blake dropped out of Tristan's movie after their fight. At least they won't be showing up. Still, it hits me again, like someone lobbed a brick at my stomach. I'm going to help Tristan with his movie. Lydia, Jake, Tina, Jack—they're all coming to hang out in our dirty, dusty, cobwebby, possibly haunted barn.

On Saturday morning, Derek is so excited that older boys are coming over *with guns* that he bounces up to check the window every five minutes. "When are they coming?" he whines each time, until my dad threatens to tie him up and throw him in the basement. Outside, the sky is a low, flat wall of gray cloud, but so far no rain. Finally, I hear gravel crunching and a car door slams. I peek out the window. It's Tristan, climbing out of a snazzy red convertible. His mother also gets out. She's svelte and gorgeous and her shoes look designer for sure. My eyes widen. She's heading for our front door!

"Come on, Mom!" I yelp. "Tristan's mother probably wants to talk to you." She's drinking coffee at the table but I grab her by the arm and drag her outside. I don't want Tristan's mother to see the corny rooster border on our kitchen walls. I also say a little prayer that she won't step in chicken poop. The thought of those designer heels getting smeared with crap makes my stomach hurt. My mother is wearing jeans and a flannel shirt, her hair scraped back in a messy ponytail, not a dot of makeup on her face. She looks great, I tell myself. She's the picture of midwestern farm life. Healthy, down-to-earth, hardworking. It's too bad they don't make designer work boots, though.

Tristan's mother introduces herself and exclaims over the wonderful house and the adorable hens and the lovely view. As far as I can tell, our view is mostly of brown, empty farm fields, since the farmers haven't planted yet. But our house sits on a small hill, and there's an old-fashioned church steeple way off in the distance. To a New Yorker, maybe that's scenic.

Tristan is carrying a big box that rattles when he walks. Toy guns. "Wow!" Derek shouts when Tristan opens the box. He dives in and grabs one. "These are so cool!" He points it at the hen coop and starts making machine gun noises.

"You can play with it," Tristan tells Derek. "Just be careful."

"Thanks!" Derek runs off, blasting away at invisible spies.

"This is perfect," Tristan says, looking around. "If it doesn't rain, we can shoot part of the scene out here, then have the gun battle in the barn. Is there enough light in there?"

"It's kind of dark, but it helps if we open up the big doors. And I have some lights you can borrow."

I lead him toward the barn. My heart is beating a little too fast and every detail jumps out at me, like I'm inside an IMAX movie—the earthy smell of mown grass, the gravel crunching under our feet, the sun glinting off Tristan's hair.

"Did you hear about Jack?" Tristan asks.

I shake my head. "Now what?"

"He got caught hanging up posters in school yesterday afternoon."

"So?"

"They were for some school event called *Nudie Monday*. Basically, telling everyone to come to school with no clothes on on Monday. Supposedly signed by Mr. Safire." He grins at me as I shake my head, laughing.

"Jack has the worst luck," I comment. "Every time he tries something, he gets caught."

"Right? That's what I told him. I couldn't believe it when he didn't get grounded. I thought for sure I'd have to postpone today."

I swing open the barn door. Inside, there's a musty, furry, old manure smell but it's faint, more like a memory of a smell than a real one. A shaft of sunlight spills in from the second-story window and cuts across the barn.

"Wow," Tristan murmurs. "You're so lucky."

Lucky? I glance at him to see if he's joking but he looks reverent, like he's in a church. He glances up at the hayloft.

It's like the barn's second story, but it's really just a big, open platform. A few bales of hay lay scattered around. My mother keeps her equipment and chicken feed in the barn. My dad uses it to store the mower and our old blue Chevy pickup. My dad calls it our country Cadillac, but I think zombiemobile is a better name. It's covered in patches of reddish rust, like some kind of weird skin disease for trucks. It's missing two hubcaps and the engine chugs and rattles like an old geezer with bad lungs. I'm hoping Tristan won't notice it, but his eyes light up as soon as he sees it. He hurries over and runs a hand along the bumper.

"Wow. What is this, like a 1970 Chevy?"

"Something like that." Actually, I have no clue.

He shakes his head and peers inside. "This is amazing."

The zombiemobile? There's no accounting for taste. "It's kind of a rust bucket," I point out.

"It needs a little fixing up, that's all. My dad's having a 1962 Ford Thunderbird restored. It's going to be pretty sweet when it's done. I told him we should do it ourselves." He rubs a speck of dirt off the zombiemobile, even though it's covered in dust. "He says it's easier to find the money than to find the time."

"I wish my dad had that problem," I say cheerfully.

"I guess." He sounds regretful, though. "Is your dad restoring this?"

I pat the zombiemobile like it's a new, favorite pet. "Well, he changes the oil every now and then."

Tristan laughs like I've said something really funny. "If he ever needs help working on it, let me know. This would be amazing if you restored it."

Outside, we hear tires crunching on gravel. Someone else has arrived.

"Tristan!" his mother calls from outside. She peers in through the barn door. The sun has broken through the clouds and it throws her huge, jaggedy shadow across the wooden floorboards.

"Whoa," Tristan and I say at the same time. We grin at each other.

"That is so film noir," I murmur.

"Totally," he agrees. "I'm using that in my movie."

"This is so adorable!" his mother calls, which ruins the scary effect. "Some of your friends are starting to show up, honey. You should come outside."

Honey? I bite my lip to keep from smiling.

"I'm coming, Mom." He rolls his eyes at me.

Parents.

Everything starts to get crazy busy. Lydia, Tina, and Emily show up as Tristan's mother hops in her car and waves good-bye. Another minivan full of kids shows up right after them. Tristan fills me in on what's going on. He's shooting his biggest scene today, where Lydia double-crosses Jack's character by telling the rival gang where he and his boys are hiding out. The gang shows up and there's a big shoot-out.

"Chickens!" Lydia screeches, as soon as she sees the hens in their outdoor pen. "I missed you!" She and Emily run over to the pen. Pretty soon they're laughing hysterically. Maybe one of the hens pooped. I should be nervous, but strangely, I don't care. I've already heard every dumb chicken poop joke there is, so why worry? Lydia turns and waves wildly to Tristan. I wait for him to run over and join them but he just waves back.

"I need a pair of earplugs when I work with those two." He says it jokingly but it makes me wonder. Maybe Tristan isn't going the Hollywood formula route after all.

Pretty soon, Tristan and I are discussing camera angles for the first shot. There are a lot of things to think about. That's why big Hollywood directors have assistant directors. They even have assistants for their assistants. It's just me and Tristan but we do a pretty good job on our own. Tristan decides to go with a high angle for the first shot of the gangsters opening the barn door. We set up the camera in the hayloft, looking down. If we get lucky and the sun comes out again, the guys in their fedoras will cast some killer long shadows across the rough floor.

Once the camera is ready, we check to see if everyone is in costume. The only person missing is Jack Timner. Tristan texts him: *Where r u?*

We tweak the lights and rehearse the scene. I stand in as Jack. It's actually kind of fun not being the director. I don't have to make all the decisions. I get to enjoy myself instead of worrying about making a mistake. Jack hasn't texted back and I can tell Tristan is getting nervous. He's about to call him when a car pulls into our driveway.

"You're late!" Tristan calls as soon as Jack opens his door.

"Jack!" Lydia shouts from over by the henhouse, like she just spotted her long-lost buddy. "Jacko! I get to slap you today! I can hardly wait!"

She and her friends head over. Something looks wrong with Jack, though. He stares at the ground, kicking at stones, as his father gets out of the car. His dad isn't real tall but he has a thick neck and burly arms and a crew cut, like he's still in the army. He glances around, looking for an adult, but Tristan's mother is gone and my parents are in the house. Mr. Timner spots Tristan and strides over.

"Jack has some news he wanted to tell you in person." He curtly nods his head to Jack.

Jack glances at Tristan and then goes back to eyeing the gravel. "I'm going to military school," he mutters.

Lydia arrives as he delivers the news. "*What?*" she practically screams. "Military school? No way!"

We all stare at Jack. What is he talking about?

"Military school?" Tristan repeats. "You mean for eighth grade?"

Jack grimaces. "I'm leaving tomorrow. It's in Indiana."

"Tomorrow!" Tristan stares between Jack and his father. "What do you mean?"

Neither one answers. Jack stares at the ground and Mr.

Timner stares at Jack. He stands, legs apart, hands clasped behind him, like he's ready to snap a salute at any moment.

"What about my movie?" Tristan asks. "We're halfway finished!"

Mr. Timner clears his throat. "Yes, we're very sorry about that. We really are. Jack's mother and I think this change will give Jack a chance to settle down and apply himself to his schoolwork."

"But there's only a month left of school," Tristan bursts out. "Why send him now?"

Mr. Timner's mouth tightens. He doesn't like being questioned. "We have to do what we think is best for Jack. We want him to finish out the year there so he has a chance to meet the other boys. He starts on Monday."

Jack's face, angled away from his dad, looks sad and mad at the same time, like he wants to punch somebody or start crying, or maybe both.

"Dude, you're leaving tomorrow?" Tristan says in a low voice to Jack. "Are you kidding me?"

Finally, Jack looks up. His face is so miserable that I have to look away. "Sorry. It's not like I want to go," he adds, an edge to his voice. "I wish I could stay."

"Are you staying today at least? Maybe we can squeeze in enough scenes to finish it up."

Mr. Timner shakes his head. "He's got a lot of packing to do so I'm afraid he can't stay. I wanted to let him tell you in person, though."

"This is going to ruin the whole movie!" Lydia says it to Jack, but of course she's really talking to his dad. Mr. Timner turns and walks back to the car. He probably thinks we all need a good dose of discipline.

And there's nothing we can do or say. We're just kids. To Jack's parents, this is some dumb little seventh-grade project that doesn't matter. The boys punch Jack on the shoulder or thump him on the back to say good-bye. Lydia, Tina, and Emily all give him a big hug. I step up to say good-bye, too. Even though Jack and I weren't close, he throws his arms around me. A warm, sour hot dog smell clings to his T-shirt. "Good luck with your movies," he says in a choked voice. "I better see your name on the big screen someday."

"I hope you will." I want to say something encouraging like that to him but I have no idea what Jack hopes to do one day. I never bothered to ask. Now I wish I had gotten to know him better. "Good luck, Jack."

He doesn't wave as the car pulls away. He just sits hunched in the front seat, staring at nothing. A strange quiet falls over our group. Even Lydia is silent as we watch the car disappear down the road.

"I can't believe it," Tristan finally says. "I cannot believe it. This sucks!" He kicks at the ground, spraying gravel.

"Military school," Lydia says. "Poor Jack."

We all nod. Poor Jack.

Tristan looks shell-shocked. I probably had the same look when I lost my mask. Everyone tries to convince him to finish without Jack but he says too many crucial scenes are missing. For a second, I wonder if I've jinxed Tristan's movie. Did the hens throw a curse on me and now I'm bad luck? After all, it seems pretty strange that first my movie, and now Tristan's, has gone down in flames. And it happened right here at my house. I glance over at the hens. They look innocent, clucking and scratching at the dirt, but I know better. Bad things seem to happen whenever they're around. Still, Jack has been getting in trouble for a while. I never thought his parents would follow through on their threat to send him to military school. I guess Jack didn't either.

Now Tristan's movie is missing its star, and my star is missing his head. Whether the chickens jinxed us, the stars crossed us, or plain old bad luck came knocking on our door, it seems that Medford Junior High's two moviemakers are sitting on the sidelines for the upcoming film festival.

After Jack leaves, a sad quiet hangs over us. Even Lydia isn't in the mood to laugh. A few kids call their parents, and pretty soon two moms with minivans cruise up. Everybody piles in except Tristan. He still has to collect his equipment, so he decides to wait for his mother to return. After the others leave, we silently walk to the barn and I help him pack up. As if on cue, the rain finally lets loose. We stand in the doorway and watch it pour. Tristan turns away, looking dejected. He would probably rather be alone. I'm sure the last thing he wants to do is hang out with me all day. Maybe I should offer him a ride. I don't think my parents would mind. I'm about to ask when he glances over. "Your first movie was about zombies, right?"

"Zombie chickens." The one you thought was really dumb, I think to myself.

His face brightens and he pushes the hair out of his eyes. "Hey, you want to show it to me?"

"What?" Panic grips me. All this time I thought Tristan was laughing at my movie and he wasn't. Now, what if I show it to him and he actually does laugh? We'd go right back to being not friends again.

"Uh, you probably don't have time," I tell him. "It's pretty long."

He flashes a sad smile. "I've got all afternoon."

My brain snaps into overdrive, trying to find an excuse not to show it to him. "If you watch it right now, it might make you feel worse. You know, with Jack dropping out and ruining your movie and everything. We should do something different."

Tristan sighs. "Actually, about the only thing I feel like doing right now is watching a movie."

"We've got tons of movies," I quickly say. "I'll show you what we have."

Tristan shoves his hands in his pockets. "I've probably already seen them. I want to see *your* movie."

I can't think of an argument for that. We run through the rain to the house and Tristan talks to my dad about the zombiemobile while I make popcorn and grab drinks. We head into the TV room and I pop in *Night of the Zombie Chickens*. My stomach is so knotted up, I can't even eat the popcorn. Tristan munches away, looking relaxed. If he thinks my movie is dumb, he doesn't let on. Sometimes he asks how I created a certain lighting setup, or he compliments an angle I picked. He doesn't scream during the scary parts, but he doesn't laugh, either. Every now and then, I glance at him out of the corner of my eye. He smiles at the part where Alyssa gets transformed by eating a zombie egg and turns into Margaret.

"Wow, nice twist. I didn't see that coming." At the end, he claps his hands.

"Shut up," I say, my face growing red. I saw every mistake and I'm sure he did, too.

"No, I mean it. That was good. Better than I expected. You know how it is. Some people tell me they made a movie and it's mostly their friends acting silly. I love your ending because it's so out there. I hate formula endings."

"Me too!" Formula endings are the biggest beef I have against Hollywood movies. Maybe we have more in common than I thought. "You have to show me your movie someday," I remind him.

He nods but he's distracted again, staring out the window. "I can't believe Jack is leaving," he murmurs. "He was one of my friends. And all that work down the tubes. Man, my parents are going to be so mad. It's a good thing they weren't here today."

"It's kind of weird, isn't it? Both our movies ending up in the trash can."

"Yeah." Tristan munches thoughtfully on popcorn. "Are you sure you can't rewrite your ending to make it work?"

"I'm still missing some key scenes. If I edited it together right now, I'd probably only have thirty-five minutes, so it's way too short."

"Too short?" Tristan gives me a funny look and then flicks a popcorn kernel at me. "Didn't you read the festival rules, dummy? Student films have to be fifteen minutes or less."

I stare blankly at him. Film festivals have rules? "I haven't gotten around to reading those yet," I admit. I can feel my cheeks growing pink. He must think I'm an idiot. "Fifteen minutes? Are you sure? That seems really short."

"They get a lot of movies and the judges have to watch them all. They don't want to watch hour-long movies from a bunch of kids." He shakes his head. "Were you really making a full-length movie? Wow, you must have been busting your butt. I can't believe it."

I can't believe it, either. I guess I have a lot to learn about film festivals. Why do I always end up looking foolish in front of him? I nervously toss a piece of popcorn into the air to catch in my mouth. Tristan is too fast. He grabs it out of the air, pops it in his mouth and grins at me. Rational thoughts scramble in my brain like egg yolks. I smile foolishly back. It suddenly feels like we're trapped in a car mirror, where objects are closer than they appear.

"Do you realize what this means?" Tristan's bright,

swimming pool eyes light up. "Kate, you probably have enough material to put something together for the festival!"

I focus with difficulty. "I haven't shot the last scene yet. It won't make sense without that."

"Maybe you just need to change your script. You know, figure out a way to end it without showing his face."

It feels like he's suggesting I dig up a two-week-old dead body and try to restart the heart. I've already given up on *Bride of Slug Man*. Could I possibly revive it? I frown at him. "I don't know. That sounds tricky."

He jumps up. The popcorn bowl teeters in my lap. "I know! Show me your footage! Maybe we can come up with an ending."

I jump up, too. The footage is on my computer, which means we'll have to go up to my room. Did I leave dirty underwear hanging on the back of my chair again? Letting Tristan view *Night of the Zombie Chickens* was bad enough. Now, he'll see my messy room. Even worse, he'll see my messy, raw footage.

"Come on, Walden," Tristan demands when I raise an objection. "So what if it's rough? Let's see if we can save it."

His excitement is contagious. My brain starts whirling. All these weeks of moping and now it turns out I might still be able to enter the film festival! That's when it hits me. Tristan's movie was ruined and it wasn't even his fault. He has a right to mope and act depressed. Instead, he's trying to help me. I feel embarrassed at how silly I've been acting.

I assumed Tristan would be a snob because he's from New York City. Instead, I've been a weird kind of reverse snob. If I hadn't been so jealous, we could have become friends. Then I might have found out about that fifteen-minute rule. I would have saved myself a lot of stress, not to mention hours of slimy hard work.

"Walden!" Tristan snaps his fingers in front of my face. "Hello?"

"Sorry. I was just . . . thinking."

With my heart pounding, I lead him upstairs. I make him wait outside while I clean up the worst of the mess. I only wish I could clean up my footage. What about all the bad takes where the camera wobbles or someone messes up? Will he think I'm a lousy director? Will he laugh at my slug man? I take a deep breath, throw open the door to my room, and Tristan Kingsley walks into my inner sanctum.

We sit down together and watch every clip. I'm afraid he'll laugh when he sees Slug Man, but he just says, "Great costume. Those are some mean-looking claws." He laughs like crazy at the footage of everyone getting slimed and he especially loves the footage of Leo. "Oh, man," he says over and over. "This guy is good. Where did you find him?" I explain the whole story and pretty soon we're both cracking up. "I'm doing my next auditions at the Crow Bar," he jokes.

Once we've watched all the footage, we sit and stare at the blank computer. "So that's it," I tell him. "I have lots of footage but there are some big holes."

"Let's make a diagram." Tristan grabs a piece of paper

and pencil and starts writing. "Okay, first scene, Slug Man arrives. Second scene, the wedding."

He goes on, writing down every scene, and then we brainstorm. I have way too much material, so we decide to shorten some of the chases and the slimings. The scenes I haven't shot yet aren't as crucial as I thought. The biggest problem is the last scene where Adrienne promises to find an antidote one day to restore Christopher. Then Adrienne and Christopher, the beauty and the beast, share a kiss and slowly walk off into the sunset.

I know, it's a little corny, but what can I say? I like happy endings.

Tristan scratches his head after he reads it. "They walk off into the sunset? You ended your other movie that way."

"I know but I couldn't think of anything better."

He gives me a pained look, like, *And you thought that was a good idea*? This time, I just laugh. "You're right, it's lame. But you see the problem. How can I end with a faceless monster?"

Tristan bites on the end of his pencil. "Yeah, the romantic ending is definitely out. You can't do romantic without a face. Why not try a sad ending? Judges love that. Like *King Kong*, where he kidnaps the woman he loves and they shoot him off the Empire State Building."

Hmm, it's not a bad idea. Tragedies are deep. That means the people who make them must think deep thoughts. Yeah. Maybe *Bride of Slug Man* is a romantic sci-fi tragedy. After a lot of brainstorming, Tristan and I come up with the absolute perfect ending. As he jots notes with a pencil, I type on the computer:

EXT: TREE HOUSE—DAY

Adrienne lies huddled on the tree house floor. The slug creature, Christopher, stands nearby guarding her. He's leaning over the railing staring at the ground.

(Luckily, we have a tree fort in our backyard, left over from the last owners. It's old and splintery but my dad pounded about a hundred nails into it and he said it should last until Derek and I are grown up and have our own kids.)

Cut to close-up of Adrienne as a claw suddenly reaches down and strokes her hair. She stares upward. The lightbulb clicks on! This is still Christopher, the love of her life, trapped inside a monster's body.

ADRIENNE

Oh, Christopher, are you still there?

EXT: FOREST HIDEOUT—DAY

Nearby, three scientists hide behind bushes, SINCLAIR, REGINALD, and DOUGLAS. They're dressed in white lab coats and safety goggles, and carry guns. Reginald peers through binoculars.

REGINALD

He's still got her in the tree. How are we going to rescue her?

SINCLAIR

He'll see us coming if we try anything.

DOUGLAS

Not if we cover his eyes. I have a plan. I'll stay here and make a distraction by firing off my gun. You two climb the tree and throw a burlap bag over his head. If he can't see, he won't be able to slime us. Then we can tie him up, carry him back to the lab, and try to cure Christopher

so he doesn't have to spend the
rest of his life as a mollusk.

REGINALD

Why don't YOU go throw a bag over
his head and *I'LL* distract him?

DOUGLAS

I'm a better shot. If anything
goes wrong, I'll shoot him.

REGINALD

(grumbling)

Fine, but this better work.

CUT TO:

Douglas jumps out and waves and fires
his gun into the air.

DOUGLAS

Hey, over here! Come and get me!

CUT TO:

Reginald and Sinclair creep toward
the tree from the rear.

CUT TO:

Close-up of Christopher the slug creature looking really mad.

(I know I have a few close-ups of Noah that I can throw in here.)

CUT TO:

Reginald and Sinclair climb into the tree house from behind, creep up on Christopher, and throw a canvas bag over his head. Christopher battles them and Adrienne screams as a stream of green goo almost hits her.

SINCLAIR

Christopher, you almost hit Adrienne! If you really love her, then stop!

The slug creature's shoulders sag and he gives up. They jump on him and tie his hands together with a rope. While Reginald checks on Adrienne, Sinclair leans close to Christopher.

SINCLAIR

I've always secretly loved Adrienne, you know. Now, she's all mine!

Christopher BELLOWS in fury. He rips off the ropes and grabs Sinclair and chokes him!

CUT TO:

Douglas takes aim with his rifle and shoots.

CUT TO:

Christopher clutches his chest as Adrienne screams. He reaches out in her direction. She reaches toward his claw, but before she can touch him, he stumbles backward and falls out of the tree house, plunging down, down, into the murky forest below. Adrienne runs to the railing.

ADRIENNE

Christopher!

FADE TO:

Reginald and Douglas stand over Christopher's slug body.

REGINALD

He was a great scientist. It's a tragedy that an alien killed him in the end.

DOUGLAS

It wasn't the alien that killed him. 'Twas amour killed the mollusk man.

They both glance up at Adrienne in the tree house, gazing down on the dead body of her lost love.

FADE TO BLACK

After I type the last word, I lean back in my chair. It's crazy, but I think it might just work. "Are you sure about Douglas's last line? Won't it sound like I'm copying *King Kong*?"

Tristan shakes his head. "It's not copying. It's an

homage." He says it like oh-MAJJ. "It's like a nod of the head, a tribute to *King Kong*. The judges will love it."

I read out loud what we've written. "It's perfect."

Tristan grins. "As perfect as it gets with a headless hero, anyway. You need to schedule the shoot ASAP. Mind if I help out?"

"Are you kidding? It was your idea."

Tristan points out the window. "Hey, look."

The rain finally stopped and golden beams of light are punching holes through the dark clouds.

"Wow," I murmur. "They're like huge spotlights."

Tristan nods. "Or tractor beams from an alien spaceship."

The world gleams wet and green and shining. The church spire in the distance glows white, like a TV antenna receiving a perfect, static-free signal from God. Maybe I do see what Mrs. Kingsley meant by the beautiful view. I feel shy standing so close to Tristan. It's like we've suddenly shared something personal, something you can't easily put into words.

Maybe he feels the same way because he looks down and fumbles with the pencil. "Okay. So." He grabs at the popcorn and ends up knocking over the whole bowl. I would almost swear he's nervous, except Tristan Kingsley never gets nervous. As we bend down to pick up the popcorn, our hands collide. He grabs mine, smiling, and circles his fingers around my wrist. One of those alien tractor beams must lock on to us because time almost stops. A bird drifts by the window, flying in slow motion. Tristan is saying something about my small wrist, but sound waves have distorted, too. All I hear is weird, alien mumbling. That, and the thudding of my heart.

Then, his cell phone goes off. He drops my hand. The tractor beam dissolves and time snaps back hard, like someone was stretching a giant rubber band and finally let it go. The jangling ringtone is so loud it makes me jump.

His mom. She tells Tristan she's almost at our house and to get ready. I practically run out of my room and he follows. I feel a little dizzy. Was he only commenting on my tiny wrist or was it an excuse to hold my hand? Did time distort for him, too, or have I watched way too many sci-fi flicks? I wish I knew what he was thinking. He stops at the front door and hands me the pencil. I stare down at it because I'm too embarrassed to look at his face right now.

"Thanks for showing me your movie."

I bob my head. "Don't forget, you have to show me yours sometime." Inwardly, I cringe. *You show me yours and I'll show you mine!* Yeesh. So grade-schoolish. I can invent a thousand zings for Paul Corbett. Why can't I come up with a single clever thing to say to Tristan?

"Sure. See you later."

"Bye." I watch through the screen door as he walks to the convertible. "Hey, Tristan!"

He turns and glances back, shading his eyes from the sun.

"Sorry again about your movie. And, um, thanks. Thanks for helping with mine."

He smiles and waves. "Can't wait for the shoot!"

I shut the door and lean against it. Neither can I.

29

On the morning of my last big shoot, everyone is supposed to show up at ten a.m. At nine forty-five, I hear the crunch of gravel outside. Who shows up fifteen minutes early on a Saturday morning?

Noah Fleming does. He stands awkwardly in the doorway to our kitchen, blinking like the light is too strong. “Doris isn’t here yet?”

“You’re fifteen minutes early, Noah,” I point out. “Sit down and read the script. She’ll be here soon.”

Doris only arrives five minutes early. I guess there’s still hope for her. Everyone else shows up late, and Tristan doesn’t show up at all. By the time Lizzy and Alyssa have hustled everybody through wardrobe, I still haven’t heard from him. Tristan told me he would supply the guns and bring along two extra boys to play the scientists, Reginald and Douglas. Now, they're all missing.

I text Tristan for the third time. Was he just pretending to be nice so he could embarrass me, like I embarrassed him? Maybe he never intended to show up. I decide not to text him anymore. For all I know, he's laughing and showing my texts to his friends. I have to make this work without him. I'll shoot the scene between Noah and Doris first, since it doesn't require guns or scientists.

To avoid seeing Noah's head, I tell him to bend over the railing and gaze at the ground below. I shoot from a low angle behind him, so all I see is his back. Then I pan to Doris lying curled up at his feet so he's out of the shot.

"Okay, Noah, reach down and stroke her head with your claw."

The claw comes into frame and strokes Doris's hair. Perfect. Now, all Doris has to do is raise her head and say her line. Instead, she yelps and slaps at the claw. "Ow, you're pulling my hair!"

I groan to myself. "Cut!"

"He's getting my hair all tangled!" Doris shouts.

"It's not my fault! It's this claw," Noah insists. "It's getting stuck."

When I touch Doris's hair, it feels like sticky plastic. Somebody got a little too happy with the hair spray. No wonder the claw got stuck. They must have sprayed half the bottle on her head. "Hair!" I call.

Alyssa runs over, smiling sheepishly. "I was afraid it might blow around too much in the wind. I'll brush through it. That should help."

"Let's get all the way through the scene this time," I tell Doris, trying to be patient. "Noah, don't stick your hand so far in her hair. It looks like you're trying to claw her brain. Just lightly touch the top of her head."

I run a hand through my own hair. It must be standing straight up because Alyssa runs over with her comb and tries to tame it.

"Never mind," I bark. "Places, everyone!"

I'm way more annoyed than I should be. After all, I'm used to doing lots of takes, and Alyssa was only trying to help. Is Tristan really going to ditch and leave me without guns or actors? I heard the film business is rough. I just figured the dirty tricks happened in Hollywood, not at Medford Junior High.

Doris and Noah take their places. The next take goes fine, except Doris looks like she's sucking on lemons when she glances at Noah. Her voice is flatter than a zombie death rattle when she delivers her line.

"Cut! Let's do it again!"

I stroll over to talk to Doris and Noah. "Now, Adrienne," I say, hoping this will remind Doris that she's playing a part. "You're scared. You think Christopher is now a monster who's going to kill you. Really, he's still crazy about you but he doesn't know how to tell you."

Noah stares up at the sky, nodding his head. I notice he's blushing. Of course. I realize that I'm not just talking about Christopher. I'm talking about Noah. I'm talking about the two of them. Romance is tough, whether you're a mollusk or a human. It's the language everybody understands but nobody is very good at. Star-crossed couples may be great for Shakespeare, but it's time to straighten these two out.

"Noah doesn't have a way to tell you how much he still cares about you," I go on.

Doris shoots me a suspicious look. "You mean Christopher."

"Of course. And even though you really like him, lately you've been treating him like you can't stand him." I pause. "Because, you know, he turned into this monster. So how do you think that makes him feel? He misses your friendship."

Doris sneaks a sideways glance at Noah. "He's changed. That's the problem. Christopher is chasing after Adrienne now, always trying to get her attention."

"That's right," I quickly say. "Christopher is trying really hard to make you like him again." I glance at Noah. "Maybe he's trying too hard."

I let this sink in. Doris is frowning at her shoes. Noah nervously bounces from one foot to the other. "So Christopher feels kind of hurt, right?" he says. "Here's this girl he likes and he thought she liked him. I mean, they got married, right? Only now it seems as if she doesn't like him but he doesn't know why, so he's trying to figure it out and maybe that's why he's pestering her." He says this all in a rush, his face turning pink.

"Who said she doesn't like him anymore?" Doris blurts. "I mean, I bet Adrienne still cares about Christopher, right? She just wants him to be himself again," she adds. Now her face is pink, too.

"If Christopher just knew that Adrienne still liked him, I bet he wouldn't act that way anymore," I say.

Noah nods to himself, staring at the horizon. "Yeah," he says under his breath.

Doris looks past him to me. "I do. I mean, you know, Adrienne does. My character does. Right?"

"Right. Exactly." I take a deep breath. Fixing their romance is all fine and good, but I still have a movie to shoot. "So, in this scene, Christopher touches your hair. It's like he's saying, look, it's still me, trapped in this other body. And you have to show him in your voice, when you say your line, that you still care about him."

I hear a muted scratching behind me. It's Alyssa and Margaret. They're precariously perched on the top step of the tree house, heads peeking over the bottom railing, bug-eyed from listening so hard. Alyssa puts a hand on her heart and wipes away a fake tear. I almost snort with laughter but manage to hold it in. "Uh, I have to fix something with my camera," I tell Noah and Doris. "Let's take five minutes. Maybe it will help if you guys talk about this scene together, okay?"

I'm on a tight schedule but I figure my day's going to go better if these two patch it up. Alyssa and Margaret are already scrambling down the steps before Doris sees them. I follow them and park myself at the bottom of the tree. Murmuring voices drift down from above. When I hear Doris's honking laugh, I know Noah must have told her another science joke, and everything must be okay.

And then, my phone rings. It's Tristan.

"Kate!" He sounds excited, or maybe frantic.

A huge surge of relief washes through me and the knot in my chest melts. He hasn't ditched me. Suddenly, I realize Margaret and Alyssa are both watching me, little smiles plastered on their faces. Margaret puts a hand to her mouth and whispers something to Alyssa like they're back in fifth grade.

"Where are you?" I say crossly, all business.

"My cell phone died," he babbles. "And I have a big problem. I got Scot Logan and Kyle McCarthy to play the scientists, but Kyle broke his arm in soccer practice yesterday and didn't bother to call me until this morning. So I've been trying to find someone else to play the part, but everybody's busy. There's one guy who says he'll do it, but I wasn't sure if you'd want to use him."

"At this point, I'll settle for anyone. Who is it?"

"Uh, well," Tristan hesitates, "it's Blake Nash."

"Blake Nash?" I shout the name in disbelief. "Are you serious?"

Alyssa, Margaret, and Lizzy all run over. They're dying to know why I'm shouting Blake's name.

"Forget it," I say right away. "If he agreed, then it's just to cause trouble. Are you two even still talking? Because I thought, you know, after the fight . . ."

"Yeah, we worked things out," Tristan says. "I asked him straight up if he was mad at you but he told me he's fine, no hard feelings. He was actually pretty good in my movie. And he's the only one I can find."

I have a bright idea. "Tristan, why don't you do it?"

He laughs. "I stay strictly *behind* the camera."

"Just this once," I plead.

"Sorry," he says firmly. "I'm doing you a favor. Blake will do a much better job."

"Let me call you back." I hang up and sink to the ground. Why would Blake Nash volunteer to be in my movie? My friends hover over me.

"What did Blake do now?" Lizzy screeches.

I explain the situation. "Tristan's waiting to hear from me. Should I say no? What do you think, Margaret?"

Margaret wrinkles her nose. "Who else could we get?"

I think about the options, which are pretty much Derek or my dad. It's hard to imagine either one paired with Scot Logan and Trevor. It would look silly. Derek is too young and my dad is way too old. The scene won't work with only two scientists. I need one to shoot the gun and the other two to wrestle with Christopher. "I don't know of anyone," I tell Margaret. "But the point is, do we want Blake around?"

Margaret pulls a blade of grass and sticks it in her mouth. "If Tristan says he won't make trouble, I guess I'm okay with it, since there's no one else."

"Why would he want to do this? It doesn't make sense. It's got to be some kind of revenge plot he and Paul have cooked up."

"Maybe Blake just feels bad about what happened, so he wants to help out," Lizzy offers.

I give a short laugh. "It's kind of late for that. I don't want him hanging around."

Margaret swats at a fly. "If Blake feels bad about everything then I think we should forgive him. Give him another chance."

I groan. "I'm going to start calling you Saint Margaret if you don't cut it out."

The thing is, Margaret is probably right. Still, it's hard to think about being nice to Blake. We don't know if he feels bad. It's just a guess. Another guess is that he can't wait to get revenge and ruin my movie.

"Fine," I mutter. "I'm giving the thumbs-up on Blake. Someone talk me out of it, please."

Nobody does. I heave a big sigh and dial Tristan's number.

Blake Nash is on his way to my house. I can hardly believe it.

"Uh, excuse me?" Doris's head pops over the tree house railing. "Are we still shooting this thing? Because Noah is getting hot in his costume."

She's worried about him. That's a good sign.

"We'll be right up," I call.

Alyssa and Margaret are still smiling at me in an annoying way. I almost wish that Tristan wasn't coming over. I feel like telling them that he probably likes Lydia. We're just buddies. Film friends. We share a hobby, that's all. Still, I'm suddenly sweating like crazy. My damp hair is plastered to my forehead. Could I have dreaded pit stains? As I raise my arms to climb up into the tree house, I do a quick check.

"Bathroom break!" I shout.

From above, I hear Noah groan.

"I'll be right back, I promise!" I race to the house, fling open the door, run upstairs, and grab my deodorant. The problem is, my mother insists I use a natural deodorant. She says the big brands all have aluminum, which might cause Alzheimer's disease. I pointed out that there aren't too many twelve-year-olds running around with Alzheimer's, but she just said one day I'd thank her. Today is not that day, though.

Suddenly, I get an idea. My dad isn't worried about Alzheimer's disease. He uses a strong men's deodorant. I hurry into my parents' bathroom, plaster some under my arms, comb my wind-spiked hair, and run back outside. When I climb back into the tree house, Noah is lying flat on the floor and Doris is fanning him with her script. He's telling some story about rats that escaped at a science fair as Doris chuckles. It looks like Adrienne and Christopher are back on track.

"Places!" Margaret calls. "Quiet on the set!"

We shoot the scene and it's film magic. Suddenly, these two have chemistry, even if it is just Doris and a claw. At least now when she gazes at the claw it looks like the owner is important to her. Just as we wrap up the scene, Tristan arrives with Blake and Scot. My heart flutters nervously as they stride across the lawn. What if Blake picks a fight or calls me by my nickname? Luckily, he keeps his head down and stares at the grass.

I can tell right away, after Blake and Scot read some lines for me, that Blake is the better actor. Tristan gives me a look, like, *Told you so.* Even though it burns me, I give Blake the bigger part of Douglas. Trevor is still Sinclair, and Scot will play Reginald. We move on to the scene where the scientists stick a bag on Christopher's head. It's fun working with Tristan again as we discuss the best way to shoot it. He gazes around the tree house and cocks his head at me. "Where do you want to put the camera?"

I pivot, looking at angles. There isn't a lot of room. Tristan suddenly leans forward, sniffs in my direction, and wrinkles his nose. Really? I'm wearing enough industrial-strength deodorant for three men, and I *still* smell?

"That's weird," he says. "You smell like my dad."

I blink. "Really? It's probably something on the breeze. One of the guys down below." I take a big step backward and pretend to check a camera position. I smell like a man. I smell like HIS FATHER. Has my dad not heard of unscented? I keep my distance from Tristan after that.

The fight scene is tricky because we can't show Christopher's head. I'm nervous about giving Blake directions. He stares at his shoes while I'm talking, digging one toe into the ground. It doesn't look like he heard a word I said, but he does exactly what I asked, and the scene works out just fine. I use low angles and shoot it so the scientists mostly block the view of Christopher. They get the canvas bag on his head right away, and after that it's easy to shoot. With Derek's help, we get shots of slime splattering around the tree house to add in later. I also get a shot of Trevor shooting the gun and another of Noah in the slug suit, the canvas bag over his head, clutching at his chest as fake blood trickles down.

It's time for the big stunt of the movie—when Christopher falls out of the tree house after being shot. It was Tristan's idea to stuff the costume to make it look real. Or at least, real enough. I run back to the house and grab towels, toilet paper rolls, clothing, anything I can get my hands on. We also stuff the canvas sack that's supposed to be over Christopher's head and tie it on to the costume. Then, we attach a long piece of fishing line and prop the stuffed costume against the railing. My camera is set up on the ground. From a distance, it doesn't look too bad.

"Okay," Tristan says, "it's showtime."

Noah stands on the ground below, out of frame, and holds on to the other end of the line. As soon as I shout "Action!" he gives a hard yank. Mollusk Man teeters a moment, the sun glints on his oiled body, and then he crashes to the ground. Perfect. Tristan and I grin at each other. "That'll look great in slo-mo," he says.

I was thinking the very same thing! "Awesome," I agree.

It's time to shoot the very last scene. I look for my actors and catch Blake gazing at me. His eyes dart away and lock on the ground. Is there something hanging out of my nose? I wipe it, just in case. Having him around makes me nervous. Still, it's my set. I'm not going to let Blake Nash intimidate me.

"Okay," I call. "Last scene. Places, everybody."

Noah puts on the slug man costume and lies down underneath the tree. Blake and Scot stand over him, while Doris climbs back into the tree house.

"Quiet on the set!" Tristan shouts.

Margaret frowns at him. It's a good thing this movie is almost done because two assistant directors is probably one too many.

It turns out Scot is a mumbler. After the fourth take, Blake rolls his eyes. "Dude, just act like we're talking about baseball. Forget about the camera. And Kate already told you three times to stop mumbling."

It sounds strange hearing Blake say my name without an insult attached to it. It must feel funny to him, too, because he ducks his head and stares at the ground some more. Scot's face is red and sweaty. He's probably afraid Blake will beat him up if he doesn't get it right. Maybe fear is a good motivator, because he does way better on the next take. The final lines belong to Blake. Luckily, he's supposed to gaze at Christopher, because his eyes seem to be frozen downward.

"It wasn't the alien that killed him," he declares, then pauses thoughtfully. "It was amour killed the mollusk man."

I pan upward as he and Scot glance at heartbroken

Adrienne in the tree house. Then I slowly tilt down and end the shot on poor, dead Christopher. I can only hope this moment arouses sympathy in the judges' hearts, and not laughter.

I draw in a deep breath. "Cut!"

That's it. My movie is in the can. I close my eyes, relishing the moment. When I open them, Tristan is grinning at me. "Go on. We're not finished until you say it."

A cool wind ripples through the leaves above us. It stirs Tristan's hair and he pushes it out of his eyes. "You're lucky," he says, with a touch of sadness. "I'm kind of jealous."

I can't think of anything to say. It seems like we should be finishing his movie, not mine. He had the better idea, the better cast, and even better motives. It turns out I've learned a lot from Tristan Kingsley. Here he is, helping me finish my movie after his got torpedoed. He isn't sulking or trying to ambush my project, or acting superior. Maybe some Hollywood directors could also learn a few things from him.

I'm careful to stand upwind of him. "Let's say it together. I never would have finished if it wasn't for you."

Tristan shrugs modestly. "Nah, this is your show."

I shake my head. "We say it together, or we stand here all night because the movie isn't finished."

Tristan smirks. "Okay, fine."

I give him a silent three-count with my hand and then, together, we shout: "IT'S A WRAP!"

Everybody cheers. Alyssa throws a can of hair spray in the air and Blake and Trevor shoot off their toy guns. Derek shouts with the rest of us, all keyed up from hanging out with the older boys. He laughs and shoots slime into the air. Tristan draws near me and I feel a crazy lurch in my stomach. I wish he would grab my hand again. He leans in close. "I was thinking maybe sometime you and I should . . ."

In that exact moment, Derek turns and squirts me full in the face. Green slime spurts into my mouth and eyes. Goo drips off my chin as I cough and sputter. I went from sharing a moment with Tristan to looking like a Halloween freak. "Derek!" I scream. "What is your problem!?"

Even Derek's little-kid brain figures out pretty quickly that this was a bad idea. He gets a scared look and turns to run. Tristan and Blake both grab him and lift him off the ground, squealing and squirming.

"What should we do with him?" Blake asks.

I'm still wiping goo off my face and spitting it out of my mouth, but Alyssa grabs the Super Soaker with an evil smile. Maybe she's remembering the time Derek slimed her "by accident." And then she lets him have it. Derek tries to shout but that only gets him a mouthful of slime. After Alyssa empties the gun, he runs off, sticky and dripping, threatening to tell our parents and turn us all in to the CIA.

My eyes are red, my hair a sticky mess. Blake grabs one of the toilet paper rolls that we used to stuff the costume and hands it to me.

"Don't worry," Tristan says. "You look fine."

I wipe off my face. "Yeah, right. I'm dripping in green condensed milk."

Tristan smiles. "Yeah, it looks good on you."

"Uh, thanks. You're a liar."

Tristan and Blake start talking baseball. What was Tristan going to ask me? The moment is gone. Now, I'll never know. I crumple soggy toilet paper in my hand. I swear, I'm going to remove Derek's face when I track him down.

Still, as I towel off my hair, I can't help smiling. Against all odds, my movie is finished. I pause again to savor the moment. A lot has changed since we started shooting. Alyssa and Margaret are packing up props, joking together like they've always been good friends. Noah and Doris have wandered away to stare at something under a shaggy pine tree—probably conducting a biology lesson. When Doris trips on a root, Noah grabs her elbow and she doesn't jerk away. Even though I can't see it, I'm pretty sure they're both blushing. Blake wins the prize for the biggest change. He's been well behaved the entire day. No one is sure what it means, but we're all relieved.

I watch as Tristan throws a stone at a tree. The nicest change is that my rival has become my friend. Maybe he wasn't ever a rival, except in my own head. From now on, I'm not going to pretend I know stuff just to sound smart. I want to avoid coming down with another case of dreaded Director's Disease. The symptoms are a swollen head, plugged ears, and a thirst for fans and flattery.

For a while, it seemed like there was no way I could finish my movie. Instead, I ended up making two this semester—one about a slug man from Mars and the other about bullies. Somehow, Blake Nash ended up in both.

I may have finished shooting my movie, but I still have to edit the whole thing together. The film festival deadline is in one week. Every day after school I run to my computer. It's tough deciding what to cut. I have to shorten the wedding scene and shave the fight. Leo gets a brief but memorable cameo. Finally, by Thursday evening, my movie is finished. With credits and music, it's fourteen and a half minutes long. Whew. I burn a DVD, fill out the registration form for the Young Filmmaker category, and stick a bunch of stamps on the envelope. Even though it's late, I run outside and put it in our mailbox, then raise the red flag so the mailman will pick it up tomorrow.

The Big Picture Film Festival takes place in mid-June. It seems like nothing happens during the last weeks of the semester except waiting for school to be over, but actually things do happen. Tristan hears from Jack. He's okay, the school's okay, he can't wait for summer vacation.

"That's it?" I ask Tristan. "That's all he said?"

We're standing at my locker, where I'm trying to decide if I should lug my extra-heavy math book to class and break my back, or tell the teacher I forgot it and possibly get a demerit. Bad back or bad grades. Doesn't seem like a great choice.

Tristan shrugs. "What else is he going to say?"

Boys. How they can spend so much time texting and not say anything is beyond me. I finally grab my math book. I may be a hunchback by age sixteen, but at least I'll be a hunchback with good grades.

That same day, I get a letter in the mail after school. The Big Picture Film Festival is pleased to inform me that my movie has been accepted and will be shown during the Young Filmmaker segment. I scream in the driveway and all the hens squawk and run around in circles. I think they must be happy for me. Immediately, I text everybody to let them know. I wasn't sure if Tristan planned to go to the festival, but he texts back right away: *Can't wait to see on big screen!*

It turns out almost everyone who was in the movie wants to go. Doris, Margaret, Lizzy, and Alyssa drive with my family into the city. Tristan's mother gives a ride to Noah, Nathaniel, Trevor, and even Blake. I feel funny because I want to sit with my parents but I also want to be with my friends. It all gets settled when my parents sit with Tristan's mother just behind us. Tristan and the boys sit directly in front of us. My dad leans forward, squeezes my shoulder, and whispers "Good luck" in my ear.

All the student films are shown in the afternoon, one after another. Some of the films from the older students are really good. Luckily, there are two awards, one for kids fourteen and under, and another for high school and college students.

The first movie is a stop motion animation about a boy who has a goat for a pet.

"How did they do that?" Margaret whispers.

"They edit lots of photos together so the figures look like they're moving," I whisper back. "Like *Corpse Bride* and *Chicken Run*."

I start to chew a fingernail. I'm already impressed. Were the judges impressed, too?

The second movie is about a girl who goes to live with her grandmother after her parents die in a car crash. The acting is really bad. Alyssa glances at me and pinches her nose. Still, it's exciting to see what other kids are doing. There's even a movie about zombies. Tristan texts me, *Yr zombie flick is better.* My blood was definitely better. It looks like the director of this movie just picked up a few bottles of ketchup and squirted it everywhere.

Finally, my movie comes on. Both Margaret and Alyssa

elbow me. I have a big grin plastered on my face through the whole thing. I keep thinking to myself, I did this. I made this. I know every expression, every look, every goof up (which I tried to hide with clever editing). It's amazing that my movie is playing in a city theater with a crowd of people watching who don't even know me.

Then it's over. Everybody claps and Tristan lets loose with a piercing whistle. We watch four more shorts and the student films are done. The lights go up and a plump young guy climbs onto the stage and thanks everyone for coming out.

"Lots of great entries," he wheezes. "It was tough, but the judges have chosen the winner of this year's Young Filmmaker award."

Alyssa grips my elbow. Margaret is wringing her hands next to me. I clutch the arms of my seat, holding my breath.

"And the winner is . . ." He pauses dramatically. "The winner is . . . *Sister Dream* by Daniela Gutierrez!"

Sister Dream? I sink down in my seat, trying to remember it. That was a strange film about a girl who dreams about her dead sister. Then it turns out maybe she's really the one who's dead. It was well done but slow, with lots of shots of the girl walking around an old house in a long, white dress, staring dreamily off-camera.

Tristan turns and rolls his eyes. "Pseudo-artistic," he whispers. "There wasn't even a plot! I don't know why judges always go for that."

"It was well done," I say, trying to be gracious. The truth is, just watching my movie on the big screen with all the other movies was enough for me.

A tall girl with shiny dark hair in a purple dress and black leggings runs up on stage. She's wearing cat's-eye glasses and dangly earrings and looks to be around fourteen. She flashes the audience a huge grin and holds up the award. A storm of applause erupts from the front of the theater. She must have brought every cousin, aunt, and uncle in her entire family to cheer her on. It reminds me that one person's loss is another person's gain. Her family looks so thrilled, jumping up and down, that I'm happy she won, even if her film didn't have much of a plot.

Afterward, Mrs. Kingsley invites us over to their house. We eat ice cream sundaes and Tristan shows us scenes from his movie that he edited together for fun. It's too bad he can't finish it because the scenes look really good.

I'm so relieved the festival is over that I decide to take the summer off. No more movies. Maybe I'll take tennis or horseback riding lessons. I'll sleep in late, go swimming, lie out in the sun, pick raspberries from the garden. No movies, no scripts, no deadlines or lost props. . . .

"Hey." Tristan sits down next to me on the couch. "So I was thinking, it was fun working on the last scene of your movie. Maybe we should work on a project together this summer. What do you think?"

He pushes back his hair and gazes at me. My mind starts

to stutter so of course my mouth does, too. "A p-project? Sure. That would be fun!"

Hey, even directors are allowed to change their minds.

Alyssa raises her hand right away. "I want to be in it."

"Me too," Margaret echoes.

Doris makes a face like she's eating sour pickle ice cream. "No weddings."

Noah giggles and spills ice cream on himself. Blake, on the other end of the couch, leans forward. "Make sure there's a part for me." He's looking right at me when he says it, and then he smiles. At me. Okay, that's weird. From the corner of my eye, I see Alyssa's head snap up. She delivers a long, hard look at Blake, then flashes me one of her know-it-all smiles. I don't even want to know what she's thinking, but somehow I already do. For whatever strange reason, Blake Nash went from hating me to liking me. Is that even allowed? Isn't there a bully's manual with rules about stuff like this?

"We could redo my movie," Tristan says. "Start over, and use Blake as the lead this time."

"That sounds like so much fun," Alyssa purrs. I'm sure she's laughing to herself, picturing me having to work with Blake. Would he drag Paul along, too?

"Sure," I answer, "or maybe Nathaniel."

Nathaniel grins at Alyssa as he wipes a glob of ice cream from his lip. I give Alyssa a so-there look. Suddenly, Tristan bumps my shoulder and grins at me. "Do you think we could codirect without killing each other?"

As I smile fuzzily back, envisioning long hot months working side by side with Tristan, I realize Blake is scowling at his ice cream bowl. He leans back in his seat and frowns at us. Uh-oh. It looks like, one way or another, my summer is going to be full of drama.

ACKNOWLEDGMENTS

I would like to say a special thank-you to:

Tristan King, for lending me his very cool name and for being my very first fan; Catherine Sajbel, for doing such a wonderful job as both an actor and the "voice" of Kate on the *KateWaldenDirects* Instagram videos; Antonio, who laughs at my jokes and boosts my spirits when most needed; Diane Swanson, my thorough and resourceful critique partner; Joann Hill, Marci Senders, and Vikki Sheatsley, who created the galactically amazing covers for both Kate Walden Directs books; Catherine Drayton, who suggested that Kate Walden should make a second movie, and created the opportunity for me to write this book; and the entire talented Disney team, who have been such a pleasure to work with. Thanks to you all!